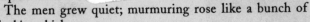

"Wait a minu...

"You're telling me... ...can't help them?"

The men grew quiet; murmuring rose like a bunch of clucking chickens.

"No need to vote." Painted Hands now remembered another reason why he chose Kiowa ways instead of the white man's. They were a stupid lot—made up rules to suit themselves and claimed to be God-fearing. In truth, they were selfish. "I'd rather bury all three of them than continue one more day with the likes of you." He whirled around and headed for his horse.

"Who's going to marry you two proper?" Sanders called. "I'm a preacher."

Painted Hands didn't attempt to hide the disgust. "How generous of you to offer your services, but I think the young woman needs to be informed since you good men are planning her future."

DIANN MILLS lives in Houston, Texas, with her husband, Dean. They have four adult sons. She wrote from the time she could hold a pencil, but not seriously until God made it clear that she should write for Him. After three years of serious writing, her first book, *Rehoboth*, won favorite **Heartsong Presents** historical for 1998. Other publishing credits include magazine articles and short stories, devotionals, poetry, and internal writing for her church. She is an active church choir member, leads a ladies' Bible study, and is a church librarian.

Books by DiAnn Mills

HEARTSONG PRESENTS

Don't miss out on any of our super romances. Write to us at the following address for information on our newest releases and club information.

Heartsong Presents Readers' Service
PO Box 721
Uhrichsville, OH 44683

Or check out our Web site at www.heartsongpresents.com

Kiowa
Husband

DiAnn Mills

Heartsong Presents

Dedicated to Roberta and Wesley Morgan

A note from the Author:
I love to hear from my readers! You may correspond with me by writing:

> **DiAnn Mills**
> **Author Relations**
> **PO Box 719**
> **Uhrichsville, OH 44683**

ISBN 1-59310-045-0

KIOWA HUSBAND

Our mission is to publish and distribute inspirational products offering exceptional value and biblical encouragement to the masses.

All Scripture quotations are taken from the King James Version of the Bible.

All of the characters and events in this book are fictitious. Any resemblance to actual persons, living or dead, or to actual events is purely coincidental.

PRINTED IN THE U.S.A.

prologue

Independence, Missouri
April 1848

"Lydia, Sarah Jane, are we ready to pull out in the morning?" Papa wiped the sweat from his brow with a dirty sleeve and sunk the dipper into a bucket of cool water for a drink.

"Very soon," Mama said. "Sarah Jane and I want to make one last check."

He leaned against the side of the narrow, canvas-covered wagon. "The sooner we leave, the sooner we get to Oregon. Is that not right, Sarah Jane?"

"Yes, Papa." She struggled to push the heavy flour sacks next to the trunk containing their clothes. Beside this rested bolts of gingham and an extra pair of shoes for each of them. Papa had decided they'd make the four- to five-month journey to Oregon, and she and Mama had been working extra hard ever since. "Do you have a little time to read me the list from the guidebook?" Sarah Jane asked.

Mama pulled the book from her apron pocket and handed it to Papa. He studied the list of suggested supplies before calling out what they needed for the journey. "Six hundred pounds of flour," he began.

Sarah Jane counted the bags. "Yes, we have them."

"One hundred fifty pounds of lard, two hundred forty pounds of bacon, one hundred fifty pounds of beans, looks like plenty of dried fruit, thirty pounds of sugar, ten pounds of salt, and twenty pounds of coffee." He peered inside the shadowed wagon. "There's the cookstove, fry pan, kettle, knives, spinning wheel, rope, axe, and my shotgun." He peered closer. "In the corner I see the grindstone, my shovel, and the water keg. Are the sewing supplies, medicine, and clothes in the trunk?"

"Along with blankets and the Bible," Mama said. "We still need to pack many of the provisions into wooden boxes on the wagon bed. I need the coop attached to the side of the wagon for the chickens, and don't forget the tar when we ford the rivers."

Despite the wearisome day, Sarah Jane felt excitement tickle her stomach. "We won't want for a thing."

"I might squeeze in my fiddle." Papa gulped the rest of the water. "What do you say, daughter?" His mustache widened with the smile beneath it. She'd never seen him so happy.

"That would be glorious. We can send merriment into the heavens. In fact, we might have a singing fest tonight."

"After the prayer meeting." Mama stared down her long nose at him. Many times she'd shared her bad feelings about the trip, and Sarah Jane had seen Mama weep on more than one occasion.

Papa wrapped his arms around Mama's shoulders. "Of course, Lydia, after we ask the Lord to bless us with safe passage to Oregon."

"And no Indians to bother us, only to trade," Mama said.

Papa glanced at Sarah Jane. "We'll say extra prayers for God to keep us safe from marauding Indians. It doesn't please me one bit that a white man, who's been raised by them heathens, is scouting for the wagon train."

Mama gasped. "Surely not! Is he Christian?"

Papa shrugged. "I'm praying the wagon master knows what's best." He glanced at Sarah Jane. "Mind you stay away from him. I don't trust him—no, not for one minute."

"Yes, Papa." Sarah Jane had seen Painted Hands. His skin was as light as Papa's and his beard the color of walnuts, but he dressed like an Indian. She'd heard he lived years with the Kiowa and committed horrible atrocities against the whites.

Sarah Jane shivered. She prayed God would keep them all in the palms of His hands.

one

Papa had warned that the hardships of traveling to Oregon would bring about the worst in the emigrants. Until today, Sarah Jane refused to believe his words. They had good friends among the folks in the wagon train. Everyone pitched in to help in times of trouble, and some evenings were filled with singing and dancing to the tune of Papa's fiddle. During the day, she often walked with the Robinson girls. If their parents knew how they giggled about the single men showing off at every opportunity, the girls would have received a good scolding; but the chatter helped ease the monotony.

"We're all marrying age," Martha Robinson, the oldest, had said three days ago. "I bet by the time we get to Oregon, we'll all have our husbands picked out. Might even be married."

"I won't." Sarah Jane nodded with her words. "I promised Papa I'd help him put in the first spring crop and harvest it before I up and marry."

"Let your new husband help," Amelia said. "How could your papa object to that?"

Sarah Jane laughed. "I imagine he'd be glad for two able-bodied people instead of one." The sound of horse hooves pounding into the prairie dirt captured her attention. Papa reined in his mare and called her name.

"I need you to drive the wagon for your mama." A frown tugged at his mustache. "She's feeling poorly."

Sarah Jane hurried back to the wagon, her heart pounding with worry over Mama. When she lifted her skirts and climbed onto the wagon seat, she inwardly gasped at her mother's pale cheeks. The journey so far had been hard on everyone, but Sarah Jane didn't mind the toilsome days, only the way Mama never seemed to be content. She seldom spoke to Papa and Sarah Jane, and she didn't show any interest in the other womenfolk, either. In a far corner of Sarah Jane's mind, she feared Mama had allowed her apprehension of the trail to possess her soul.

Since they'd crossed the Kansas River and headed in a northwest direction, the wagon train had battled hailstorms, lightning displays that lit up the sky as though God had torched the heavens, and the ever-present flash floods. Once a piercing crack of thunder had sent over fifteen hundred head of cattle stampeding into the night. The wagon train lost two days rounding up the cattle and burying four people who had gotten in the way of the frightened animals. The unpredictable weather and the hand of death trailed them all the way to the Platte River, a little over three hundred miles across the prairie. They'd passed two landmarks, according to the wagon master—Courthouse Rock and Scotts Bluff—and in a matter of days, they'd pass Chimney Rock, which marked five hundred miles from Independence, Missouri. From there they'd move on to Fort Laramie at the foothills of the Rockies. Fortunately, they could rest a little before heading on across the mountains. It was mid-June. Good timing, according to the wagon master, to beat the snowfall in the treacherous Rockies.

One night, after a little boy riding on the tongue of a wagon fell under the wagon wheels and died, she heard the wagon master, Charles Greenham, make a statement. "We're averaging one person dead every eighteen miles."

Papa had turned to Sarah Jane, more serious than she'd ever seen him. "Should we head back, daughter? I have money to purchase another farm."

"But where are your dreams?" Knowing Papa's growing concern for Mama, she added, "Mama will love Oregon. I'm praying for her every day."

Now, as Sarah Jane took the reins from Mama, she wondered if Papa had been right. Mama looked frail, like a fine piece of delicate china ready to shatter. Gazing into her once sparkling brown eyes reminded Sarah Jane of a cloudy sky— no hope or joy, only the anticipation of one more dismal day. Perspiration dotted Mama's forehead, and the morning had barely begun.

"Mama, why don't you sleep for a while? I'm sure you'll feel better soon."

"I should drive the wagon." Mama's breathing came in short gasps. "You already cook the meals and do the washing and mending."

Sarah Jane smiled into her mother's face. If not for both hands steadying the reins, she'd have hugged and kissed her. "I don't mind. When you're feeling better, we'll do the work together."

Tears welled up in Mama's eyes, and her lips quivered. "I hope so. I'm ready to feel better. I'm ashamed of the bitterness and complaining. My family deserves my best." With those words, she crawled beneath the canopy of the wagon onto a straw-filled mattress and drew the front flaps into a pucker.

Sarah Jane tried not to dwell on Mama's failing health but rather on her encouraging words. Perhaps a little peppermint tea and some castor oil would add color to Mama's cheeks. She used to laugh and urge Papa to play his fiddle and sing. Those days and weeks vanished when the wagon train pulled out of Elm Grove, a mere thirty-three miles outside Independence.

Sometimes she allowed herself to dream about happier days in Nebraska. They'd all left behind treasured friends and cherished memories, but Sarah Jane felt the same enthusiasm as Papa about the Oregon territory. She loved singing the trail songs and dreaming about the beautiful land awaiting them over the mountains.

When she thought about it, Mama had endured several difficult weeks. First Papa decided he wanted to open a mercantile in Independence. He felt that, with the wagon trains heading for California and Oregon, he'd get rich in no time at all. Once they arrived in Independence, something took over Papa, and all he talked about was Oregon. Then he decided that's where he wanted to live. Sarah Jane looked at the situation as an adventure, but Mama had lived enough days on the trail to want a home of her own. To her, Papa shouldn't have dragged them all the way from Nebraska to Missouri, then back out onto the prairie again.

He traded their heavy Conestoga wagon for a lightweight, narrower one and purchased four oxen for the journey and fifty head of cattle. They'd have fresh milk along the way, and he imagined they'd find a way to churn butter, too. Papa claimed bountiful friends awaited them in the parade of wagons and even more once they arrived in the new territory. He planned to have a small farm on the free land, then open a mercantile. A twinge of excitement fluttered through Sarah Jane, but first Mama must get well.

The day wore on. Mama began to moan in her sleep, and once she called out for Papa. The delirious cries intermingled with the creaks of the wagon wheels, prompting Sarah Jane's prayers. Anxiety rose with the prairie heat. The familiar sounds of bawling cows and the shouts of men echoed against her fears. She hadn't seen Papa for quite a while, and she needed him—his wide smile and reassurance. If only someone would ride by, she could ask them to fetch him.

Painted Hands came into view, the man Papa didn't trust. He rode alongside her as if escorting the wagon. Nervousness snaked up her spine. If Papa saw the scout, he might think she was encouraging him. Sarah Jane studied Painted Hands through the corner of her eye, a formidable man dressed in buckskin. He wore his walnut brown hair parted down the middle and tied on both sides with pieces of rawhide woven with brightly colored beads. If he'd have looked more like a white man or ridden a horse other than a spotted one, perhaps she wouldn't have trembled so.

"Miss Benson," he said, his words slow and distinct.

She turned toward him and willed her nerves to steady. Just as Papa had described him, he showed no trace of emotion. "Yes, sir."

"Can you tell me where I might find Mrs. Benson?"

"She's resting right now." Sarah Jane moistened her lips. "Have you seen my papa? I need to talk to him."

"Your father is why I'm here."

Sarah Jane weakened while her heart drummed in her chest. "Is something wrong, sir?"

He rode a little closer, and for the first time, she saw his eyes, blue like a cloudless sky, and they looked calm, not at all wild or evil. "Your father seems to have taken ill. He fell off his horse. Mr. Greenham and a few other men are with him now, but he needs to rest in the wagon."

She squeezed the reins until the leather dug into her palms. Without another word, she pulled out of the line of wagons and followed Painted Hands. *Please, Lord. Let Papa be all right. With Mama sick and Papa not faring well, this is more than I can bear.*

Up ahead, Papa's horse, a fine chestnut mare, stood with no rider. Some men had dismounted their horses and hunkered over a man lying on the ground. *It must be Papa.* The oxen moved at such a slow pace when she needed to tend to her father. Sarah Jane willed herself to stop thinking the worst. Perhaps he'd gotten too much sun.

Painted Hands swung back alongside her. "Easy, Miss Benson. I'm sure your father will be fine."

"Do you know what's wrong?" she asked.

"He's feverish. Mr. Robinson said he complained of a bad headache before he fell off his horse."

Her thoughts tumbled into more prayers. Too many folks had not survived illnesses along the way. "Sir, what do you think it is?" she asked.

"I'm not sure. The sun could have gotten the best of him."

Although she had considered the same thing, something

told her Painted Hands knew more than he claimed. Despite the heat, a chill raced up her arms as though warning her of what she'd find. At the site, Mr. Greenham helped her down from the wagon.

"Where's your ma?" he asked.

Sarah Jane avoided his gaze. "She's resting in the wagon." Suddenly, the dirt and dust from the trail settled on her lips, or was the strange sensation sweeping over her impending adversity?

Her gaze flew to where Papa lay so still on the hard ground that she feared he'd died.

"Miss Benson," Mr. Greenham said. "Your pa's real sick. I'll help him get into the wagon, and then the committee needs to meet."

She glanced up. "What do you mean?"

"Look closer. See for yourself."

Kneeling beside Papa and blinking back the tears, she searched his pale face. His closed eyes and faint breathing alarmed her. She held her breath. He was unconscious.

"Has he been feeling poorly?" Mr. Greenham asked.

"No, sir." Her mind raced. "Well, Papa's been tired and hasn't felt like eating—been fretting over Mama."

"This doesn't look good. Might be contagious." He nodded at the wagon. "I'd best take a look at your ma." He strode to the rear of the wagon while Sarah Jane stayed beside her father. She lifted his hot hand into hers—waiting, praying, willing Papa to open his eyes and speak to her.

The thud of boots alerted her to Mr. Greenham's return. "Your mother's unconscious, too. She's breathing powerful hard."

A lump rose in Sarah Jane's throat. "I need to go to her."

"Miss Benson, you've got your pa to look after, too. Do you feel all right?"

His callused words angered her. "I'm fine, and I can take care of Mama and Papa."

Mr. Greenham rubbed his graying beard. "Miss, let's get

your pa inside before any of these other folks stop to help." A couple of additional men rode their way. "We have this handled," he called. "Thanks for offering."

Painted Hands dismounted. "I'll help you. Miss Benson doesn't need to get any more worn out."

"You're most likely right." Mr. Greenham pushed back his hat. With Painted Hands, they carried Papa to the wagon and laid him beside Mama.

"Thank you," Sarah Jane said. "I'm sure they'll be fine in a few days." She walked around them to the wagon front. "I have some medicine."

"Miss Benson, you need to stay right here. I don't need healthy folks coming down with fever. After the committee decides what's best, I'll be riding back."

Again he'd mentioned the committee—the group of ten men who'd been elected before the wagons crossed the Kansas River. They served as judges and jury on the journey to Oregon. Realization settled on her heart. "Are you thinking of leaving us out here?"

Again the wagon master tugged at his beard. "I'm responsible for getting these people to Oregon safely. No one will get there if everyone's wiped out in an epidemic."

"But you don't know if what Mama and Papa have is really bad."

He peered at her a moment. "How old are you, Miss Benson?"

"Seventeen, sir."

"I recollect a good many women your age are married with families. I'll be expecting you to act respectful of the committee's decision. I'll gather the men together for a meeting at noon."

Sarah Jane stared at the wagon master. With no more words between them, she knew the verdict would be against her. These fine people who sang and danced to Papa's fiddle would leave her behind without thinking twice about her plight.

"Will you be all right?" Painted Hands asked.

Startled, she swung her attention to the Indian scout. "I believe so. I have water to cool them off. I can make a broth—and medicine—" Embarrassed at rambling, she took a deep breath. "We'll be fine."

She followed Painted Hands's gaze to the other wagons rolling by. Women and children asked what was wrong, but she only waved back. The Benson wagon trailed near the end, and she'd soon be alone.

"I'm not afraid," she said and lifted her chin.

He nodded and mounted his horse. Together, Mr. Greenham and Painted Hands rode ahead, no doubt to summon the ten men who'd decide the Benson family's fate.

Lord, I lied to Painted Hands. I'm scared, real scared.

two

Painted Hands kept his distance from the ten men who would settle the fate of the Bensons. Most of them were as skittish as new colts when he stood in their midst. His buckskins, moccasins, beaded hair, and knowledge of living in the wilderness seemed to intrigue and frighten them at the same time. He'd heard the barbaric stories of how he'd murdered innocent folks, and he'd chosen to let them believe the lies. The Kiowa ways had become a part of Painted Hands.

He understood the grave matter before them. These men had been entrusted with the burden of justice and well-being for the people of the wagon train. To allow the Bensons to continue endangered everyone, including their own families. To leave them behind meant certain death. He doubted if Mr. and Mrs. Benson would survive the fever. To Painted Hands, their shallow breathing marked a clear indication that death would soon claim their spirits. He'd seen the fever before, a sickness that knew neither age nor gender when it came to claiming lives. Typhoid fever. Painted Hands well recognized the symptoms.

"What do you think ails the Bensons?" one man asked Greenham.

"Like I said before—fever, no appetite, and just plain tired," he replied. His graying hair and weathered skin amounted to more than a small token of wisdom, and those under his charge valued his words.

"Do you think it's smallpox?" The same man spoke the dreaded plague softly, as though saying it made it true.

"No, absolutely not," Greenham said. "They don't have spots. I have a good idea, though. I've seen enough cases of them."

"Then tell us," the same man said. "We have a right to know."

"What if it's an epidemic that could wipe us out?" another man asked. "Do we want our families sick and dying?"

"I'll tell you what I think, and Painted Hands agrees with me," Greenham said. "We ain't doctors. We could be wrong, but it looks like typhoid."

A hush fell over the men.

"I'm a Christian man," another man said. "I'd hate to leave them folks out here to die when we could have done something to help."

"We're here to vote on that matter." Greenham stared into the faces of the committeemen. "We need to get this taken care of now. How many of you vote for the Bensons to leave the train?"

Some of the men talked among themselves. A heated discussion rose between a man who wanted the family to stay and another who felt it best for the Bensons to lag behind. Typhoid was a cruel master.

"Quarreling won't solve a thing." Greenham raised his voice. The men quieted, and seven of them raised their hands. A grim look deepened across his brow. "All right—I'll let their daughter know."

Painted Hands couldn't keep the sad face of Sarah Jane Benson from his mind. She was young and naïve, destined to die on the lonely trail. Earlier, her haunting green eyes had pierced his soul when she attempted to sound brave. He admired that trait, especially when weeping and regret would not solve the problem. She stood apart from the other young women with her hair the color of sun and red clay. Loose curls framed her face, and when she walked, the prairie wind teased her hair like wildflowers tossed side by side. And the freckles, the same color of her hair, disguised her womanhood with the look of a child. Unfortunately, her innocence was about to be taken by the committee's verdict.

"Are we going to leave anyone with them?" Mr. Robinson,

a hearty man, asked. "Looks to me like we're nailing down all of their coffins. If not for my family, I'd offer."

"I like that idea. And who would be volunteering?" Greenham asked.

"We'd be fools," Sanders said. He was a thin wisp of a man with a soul to match. "Whoever stays will get that fever and die; then one of us has to look after the families left behind."

"Aren't you our preacher?" Greenham asked.

Sanders stepped back. He'd just condemned himself.

"Robinson has a point," Greenham said. "Do any of you feel led to stay with the Bensons? You can join up later."

No one volunteered. The thought of Sarah Jane nursing and burying her parents set hard on Painted Hands's mind.

"We've got loved ones who need us," another man said. "I agree with Preacher Sanders."

Greenham shook his head. "So that's your vote? The Benson wagon is cut, and none of you fine men plans to stay with them." When no one commented, he continued. "I'll be riding out to the Bensons."

"If God heals them folks, then they're welcome back," Sanders said.

Now he talks of God? I don't hear of grace or mercy. Painted Hands refused to still the anger rising in him. He knew why the men made their choice, but he didn't have to agree with it. "I'll stay with the Bensons." Painted Hands stepped forward. "Greenham taught me about scouting, and I can catch up with the wagons when the sickness is over."

Silence fell around the small group. He had no intentions of asking for their permission—didn't matter anyway. He'd made a decision just as they had.

Sanders cleared his throat. "I don't approve—a young woman with a single man. Looks bad."

A knot twisted in Painted Hands's stomach. "Greenham just asked for volunteers."

"But he didn't mean single men." Sanders shook a bony

finger at him. "The Bible says for folks not to be led into temptation."

"It also says, do not kill." Painted Hands sensed the old familiar hatred churning through his stomach. He moved closer to the skinny form of Sanders. "Your vote to leave these folks most likely sends them to their death, but if a single man offers to help, that's a sin? Sounds like you're a hypocrite to me."

"What do you know about the Bible?" Sanders clenched his fists.

Painted Hands sneered at the pitiful creature before him. "Looks like a sight more than you do."

"That's enough!" Greenham raised his hand. "If Painted Hands wants to help these folks, that's his business. He knows this trail, been through it four times before. I can lead and scout this train all the way to Oregon if I have to."

"Take a vote," Sanders said. "I say if we leave him behind, then he must marry the Benson girl proper." He turned to face the other men. "What do you say?"

"All right—we'll take another vote." Greenham expelled a labored breath. "We need to get back on the trail, and this bickering is doing nothing but slowing us down."

"Wait a minute," Painted Hands said. "You're telling me that I have to marry Miss Benson or I can't help them?"

The men grew quiet; murmuring rose like a bunch of clucking chickens.

"No need to vote." Painted Hands now remembered another reason why he chose Kiowa ways instead of the white man's. They were a stupid lot—made up rules to suit themselves and claimed to be God-fearing. In truth, they were selfish. "I'd rather bury all three of them than continue one more day with the likes of you." He whirled around and headed for his horse.

"Who's going to marry you two proper?" Sanders called. "I'm a preacher."

Painted Hands didn't attempt to hide the disgust. "How generous of you to offer your services, but I think the young woman needs to be informed since you good men are planning her future."

"Let's ride there together," Greenham said. "You men go on home. I think you've made enough decisions for one day."

Painted Hands grabbed his horse's reins and swung himself up onto the saddle. He couldn't get away from Sanders and the rest of the committeemen fast enough. Marry Sarah Jane Benson? What was he thinking? All of this because he felt sorry for the family? He knew how most folks felt about him. He lived somewhere in the world between Kiowa and white man, and the Indian side of him rubbed them like fleas in a blanket. Sarah Jane wouldn't be any different. She'd choose to take care of her folks without his help instead of marrying him. No doubt her folks had warned her about him before the wagon train left Independence. He wondered which she'd fear more, the sickness or being bound to him for life.

Images from the past floated through his mind. His brothers, the Kiowa, saved him from a tragic fire that killed his parents, three sisters, and a brother when he was six years old. That fire permanently scarred his hands and earned him his name. Painted Hands loved his life with the Kiowa, but soldiers removed him at the age of sixteen and placed him in the home of the Reverend Crandle, a godly man who lived and loved his faith. The Crandles lived near Independence and were childless. They doted on him with all the devotion they would have given to their own son. From the Reverend Crandle, Painted Hands learned about God.

Painted Hands embraced the Christian faith, but unhappiness with the white people caused him to abandon God, His commands, and His Word. At the age of eighteen, he learned his Kiowa family had been killed in a military raid. Anger and bitterness, plus confusion as to where he belonged, confronted him every day. He left the Crandles, and for four years, he'd helped guide Greenham's wagons over the prairie and mountains to Oregon.

Prior to leaving Independence this last time, the Reverend Crandle told him about his brother, Jacob, who had survived the fire and settled in Willamette, Oregon. Painted Hands hoped his brother was a key to the past and hope for the future.

"You don't have to do this," Greenham said once they were beyond earshot of the wagons. "I wouldn't blame you for riding as far away from this group as you can get. I say they're crazy. In fact, this is the last wagon train I'm leading. I'm tired of dealing with all the troubles."

Painted Hands laughed. "It's my last." He paused. "Miss Benson may be repulsed at the idea of marriage."

"I know, but she'd be foolish to turn you down. You're a fine man, Painted Hands, and I've been honored to make your acquaintance and work with you these past years."

Painted Hands whipped his gaze toward the wagon master. Greenham rarely did much more than bark orders, but Painted Hands respected him. "Thank you."

"I meant every word. I can see you're torn between living as an Indian or a white; but either way you decide, the other side loses."

&

Sarah Jane paced along the outside of the wagon. She'd washed down Mama and Papa with cool water and tried to get them to drink ginger tea, but neither one could swallow it. They drifted between sleep and unconsciousness, both eaten up with fever and delirium.

She stared in the direction of the wagon train and pondered the committee's decision. Deep within, she sensed the lone wagon would be abandoned. And she understood their way of thinking. They had families who faced enough danger without adding an epidemic. She sighed and crossed her arms over her chest in an effort to ease the aching in her heart. *What am I going to do? What can I give Mama and Papa to stop the fever? How long will they be sick? What if they don't survive?*

The thought of burying them or getting the fever caused her

to shudder. When would Mr. Greenham be here? Not knowing left a queasy feeling in the pit of her stomach. How could she settle things in her mind with such an uncertain future?

She studied the outline of two riders heading her way. One part of her wanted them to hurry, and the other part dreaded the decision.

"Please don't let them abandon us, dear Lord," she whispered. "I don't know what I will do." She swiped at a tear. Mr. Greenham and Painted Hands would not see her cry.

She checked one more time on Mama and Papa before the two men arrived. She prayed to see them awake and her fears arrested, but their condition had not changed. She dabbed the perspiration on their faces and offered another prayer before stepping from the wagon and hearing their fate.

Mr. Greenham and Painted Hands dismounted and led their horses toward her. Sarah Jane searched their faces for signs of a good word. Both men were stoical.

"What did they say?" She rubbed her hands together, anxiety weaving cobwebs in her mind.

Mr. Greenham cleared his throat. "Miss Benson, I hate being the bearer of bad news, but the committee feels it's best if you don't join back up with the others until your parents are better."

She swallowed her tears while a simmering of anger started to rise. "So we're left to fend for ourselves."

"You won't be alone," Mr. Greenham said.

I know God is with us. . . .

"Painted Hands has volunteered to help you through this troublesome time."

She focused her attention on the scout, not sure what to say, not sure if she should be grateful or terrified. Stories whispered around the campfires wove an unknown path through her bleak future, but Mama and Papa's care came first.

"I appreciate your help, sir. I admit I'm at a loss as to what plagues my parents."

"We think we know the cause of the fever, Miss Benson," Painted Hands said.

Sarah Jane glanced from him to the wagon master. "Please tell me."

Mr. Greenham removed his hat. "Typhoid. Painted Hands and I are in agreement."

Chills rolled over her. Typhoid killed. Her mind roared with the deadly implication. They must be wrong. Another realization struck her, and she centered her attention on Painted Hands. "You could very well get this by helping me."

Not a muscle moved on his face. "I fully understand the risk."

If she could simply read the man's eyes, see how he truly felt, learn his motivation for wanting to help. "As soon as they are better, then we can join back up with the wagons?" she asked.

"I see no reason why you can't continue with the others," Mr. Greenham said. "But the committee will have to vote again. They did have one specific request."

"I'm confused. What else am I supposed to do? Burn the wagon or pay a fee?"

Mr. Greenham hesitated.

"I'll tell her." Painted Hands looped his thumb in the top of his buckskins. "In order for me to stay with you, the committeemen say we must marry. They claim it's not fitting for a single man and woman to travel together."

A murderer. He ate his victims. Dear Lord in heaven, those things can't be true! She struggled to maintain her composure. "But they'll leave us alone to die? What if I refuse?"

Mr. Greenham touched her shoulder. "Painted Hands would still stay with you, but you couldn't join the wagons."

Bewilderment and helplessness twisted around her heart. If she'd been given to a sensitive constitution, she'd have fainted to avoid thinking about the committee's ultimatum. Marriage to Painted Hands? What would Papa say when he recovered? He'd be so angry that he might never forgive her. Sarah Jane held her breath. If the scout didn't help her, Mama and Papa would die for sure. This way they had a chance, and for them, she'd do anything.

"I'll marry Painted Hands." Sarah Jane swallowed so hard she nearly choked. She peered into her husband-to-be's face. "Thank you, sir, for your kindness. I appreciate the sacrifice you're making to help me and my folks, and I'll forever be indebted to you."

Painted Hands kept his impassive stance. This man before her had committed to spending the rest of his life with her, and she knew not why. She had neither the time nor the wisdom to discern his reasons.

Mama and Papa used to laugh and talk. For hours they'd sit in front of their sod house back in Nebraska and talk about everything from the farm to deadly twisters to the scriptures. Sarah Jane had always dreamed of the same qualities in a man. The scout before her held no resemblance to Papa. He could be spiteful, looking forward to hurting her once they were alone. Dare she live a life so miserable?

With a shudder, she realized the thoughts seizing control of her mind were selfish. Mama and Papa had given their best to her, and now she repaid their love and devotion with worrisome concerns about herself. She would honor her husband and nurse her parents back to health.

If she could only calm her quivering heart.

three

With trembling fingers, Sarah Jane removed her soiled apron and attempted to smooth back her wayward curls, damp with perspiration. Glancing at her hands, she saw they were dirty and wiped them the best she could on the apron. Tossing it to the ground, she'd gather it up after the ceremony.

I'm about to marry, and I don't even have clean hands or a clean dress.

With unsteady legs, she walked alongside Painted Hands to the spot where Mr. Sanders awaited them. She and Mama had talked about her wedding day since she was a little girl—and none of this resembled their aspirations. Certainly not the groom. Certainly not these circumstances. And certainly not while Mama and Papa lay so gravely ill.

Painted Hands avoided looking at her, and she couldn't criticize him for it. The thought of beginning her married life with a stranger filled her with emptiness. Surely he must feel the same dread, as though judged and sentenced. She knew of couples who married sight unseen and parents who arranged marriages, but this had never been a consideration for her.

"We need to get on with this," Mr. Sanders said. He opened his Bible and read the story of Adam and Eve so fast that she could barely understand him.

Sarah Jane tried to concentrate on Mr. Sanders's reading of the vows. Her mind wandered to what the Robinson girls must be saying about her fate.

"Miss Benson," Mr. Sanders said, obviously irritated. "Do you take this man to be your husband? I've asked you twice before."

The idea of crumpling into a pool of emotion held merit, but she could not. Would not. "Yes. . .yes, I do."

"I know your folks are sick, but you are making a promise to God here, and I advise you to pay attention. The wages of sin is death."

Suddenly, Sarah Jane realized how much she detested Mr. Sanders. Her God and his were not the same. "I understand God's Word quite well, and I pray for your enlightenment as well."

෴

Painted Hands fought hard not to release his temper on Sanders. The self-righteous preacher refused to venture toward the Benson wagon for fear he'd contract typhoid and demanded Sarah Jane and Painted Hands walk several yards for the marriage ceremony. Painted Hands itched to lay his fists on the bony man's jaw and leave him sprawling in the dirt.

Greenham agreed to stay with the sick couple while Sanders married Sarah Jane and Painted Hands. Even then, the preacher shifted from one foot to the other and rushed through the ceremony in the time it took to breathe in and out.

Unlike the Reverend Crandle, the man who wore the peace of God on his face and God's love in his heart, Sanders interpreted the Bible according to his whim. The preacher might be surprised at how much Painted Hands knew about the Bible, even if he hadn't found the words meaningful to his life.

Anger chiseled at his good sense every time Painted Hands recalled the callous approach of so many men toward the Bensons.

"Cut their wagon."

"We have our own to think about."

The real believers on the wagon train recognized the burden of typhoid and yet were willing to take a risk to help. Mr. and Mrs. Benson had been among these folks for days, and the others were bound to get the sickness no matter where they situated themselves. Painted Hands vowed never to forget the believers' kindness. They brought food, blankets, herbs, and prayers for Sarah Jane. Those men reminded him of some of the folks back in Missouri, who were gentle and good when the situation called for it but strong and determined when righteousness required a firm stand.

Beside him, Sarah Jane quivered so that the skirt on her dress shook. Painted Hands wished something else could have been done to help her and her parents. She feared him and rightfully so. His looks and mannerisms set him apart as a man to avoid, one with a sordid past. He heard one toothless old man state that Painted Hands murdered a whole family, but no one could prove it. Another tale drifting through the wagons told of him living with wolves and drinking the blood of the animals' prey. As soon as he and Sarah Jane grew more acquainted, he'd tell her the truth about those tales—not the vicious lies concocted by waddling tongues.

He hoped she wasn't the type of woman who made useless prattle or pestered folks with questions. He'd grown used to listening to the sounds of nature—the quiet of earth, the songs of birds and insects. There his spirit calmed the restless part of him that remembered his dark secret. Maybe in finding his brother, Jacob, Painted Hands would find peace.

Jacob was two years older, a lively boy who loved to hunt and fish. The Reverend Crandle found out Jacob had escaped the flames and run to get help. All these years, and at last, Painted Hands had found a link to his real family. Some memories had been blocked out about that night; others forged ahead like heavy boots in a muddy riverbed. He wanted to pull his feet out of the muck, but they'd been stuck for longer than he cared to remember. Some days he looked forward to the reunion with his brother. Some days he dreaded the image of a grown man calling him brother, then accusing him of murder. The screams of his family trapped inside the burning cabin preyed on his heart like a stalking cougar.

Among the Kiowa, the medicine men had tried to rid Painted Hands of the nightmares, but always they came back, each one worse than the last.

Painted Hands stared into his wife's young face. He beheld a distinct loveliness about her. He'd noticed her before because she always seemed to be laughing. He liked the part girl, part woman look about her, a combination of innocence and wisdom. Dare he hope they might grow to be friends? He didn't expect a real marriage between them. Sarah Jane already feared, maybe even loathed, him. Right now, she looked like a frightened deer. Why make the relationship any worse by consummating their vows or letting her inside his heart to learn the wretched truth?

"Most folks give the preacher something for marrying them," Sanders said, stretching out his hand.

Painted Hands considered the statement with as much gratefulness as a rattler's bite. "I'll make sure you keep your scalp."

Sanders snapped his Bible shut and headed toward his mule. "May God have mercy on your heathen soul, Mr. Painted Hands."

He wanted to take a few long steps to the preacher and wipe the smirk off his face, but he contained himself with Sarah Jane before him. He stole a look at her, and she pressed her lips firmly together. No doubt she agreed with Sanders.

"Miss Benson, we should get back to your folks," Painted Hands said.

She lifted her chin and gave him a faint smile. "I'm Mrs. Painted Hands now, and my given name is Sarah Jane."

"Yes, ma'am."

"I. . .want to thank you for all you've done." She lifted her shoulders with a deep breath, and a few, yellow-red curls slipped from under her bonnet. "I'll do my best to be a good wife."

Touched by her kind words, he wanted to respond with the same tenderness, but instead, a haunting voice rose in him— one that said she'd trick him, use him, despise him like all the other whites. Painted Hands kept his stance. He'd not be made to look like a fool. Sarah Jane needed him to nurse her parents, nothing more. When Mr. and Mrs. Benson recovered or died, she'd be on her way and he'd venture on to Oregon.

"I'm not expecting anything. We were both forced into this because of the committee. I won't be taking advantage of you."

She stepped back. Her eyes full of apprehension. Good, Sarah Jane needed to keep her distance. In the next moment, he decided not to tell her the truth about the gossip. Let her think what she wanted. He cared neither way.

four

Long after dark, Sarah Jane bedded down beneath the wagon for a precious hour of sleep. Papa's fifty head of cattle surrounded the wagon, and they acted uneasy. Maybe they sensed the trouble from the wagon train. Painted Hands and Mr. Greenham had separated them from the large herd and driven them back. The smell of the cattle almost felt comforting, as though nothing had changed.

Painted Hands had stacked his provisions in the wagon alongside Mama's spinning wheel, although he'd sold about half of them to Mr. Robinson. The day's troubles thundered in her ears, and a tear slipped over her cheek.

She prayed for God to multiply the time she slept before she crawled back into the wagon to nurse Mama and Papa. From here, the sounds from inside the wagon were vivid. If Mama or Papa rolled over or called out, she'd hear them. They drifted in and out of consciousness and often cried out from a confused world. Sarah Jane attempted to comfort them, only to realize they didn't know or care she tended at their side.

Exhaustion seized Sarah Jane's body and mind. The day had been harder than the ones before, and the fever tearing through Mama and Papa caused a longing she couldn't describe. How could one day hold so much turmoil? This morning she woke with a prayer on her lips for Mama to renew her health. Tonight she prayed for Mama and Papa's healing—and for strength to endure her marriage to Painted Hands.

In all her girlish dreams, she'd never anticipated a wedding like today's. Mr. Sanders spoke the words that sealed her to Painted Hands until death met them face-to-face. Her husband said they were forced into marriage, and he didn't expect anything in return. Sarah Jane knew precious little about married couples, but what she did know bewildered her. To be relieved of wifely duties came as a blessing when her every waking moment centered on Mama and Papa's care. Except. . .what would the future bring?

Again she worried about Papa when he learned about the circumstances surrounding her marriage. She'd seen him enraged only twice: once when a man in Nebraska beat his wife and the second time when a twister destroyed their crops. The memory of unbridled anger made her cringe. Surely he'd understand. Of course he would. Staring up at the wagon bottom, she wondered when Painted Hands planned to sleep—and where.

Tears slipped unbidden from her eyes and slid over her cheeks. Papa always said God allowed things to happen for a reason—and a good reason for folks who loved Him. *Why this? What good could come from Mama and Papa suffering with typhoid?* If the wagon train traveled at the same fifteen miles per day, how would she and Painted Hands catch up once they could travel again? They must get to the mountains before the winter snows, and every day lost weakened their chances. Would Painted Hands remain as her husband, or once Mama and Papa regained their health, would he ride out?

Oh, how she ached for release from this burden of not knowing or understanding the future. On the farm in Nebraska, Papa set traps for wolves. The sight of an animal's foot caught and bleeding in the snares of metal jaws and their mournful cries tore at her heart. Now she understood how the wolves felt; only her bleeding came from the inside.

Sarah Jane turned to stare into the fire. Painted Hands sat there on the hard ground with his legs crossed, motionless, gazing into the embers as though spellbound. She observed him, this strange man who had promised to love and cherish her. How could he maintain no emotion during all of this? His life had been changed forever, too. She wished she could master the same non-feeling demeanor. Maybe in doing so she'd grow numb and not suffer any of the pain.

Studying him closer, she saw he was a little taller than most men, stocky with broad shoulders. He wore a heavy beard along with his long, beaded hair, which most likely caused more folks to fear him. And his hands—they'd been burned and scarred. The discoloration must be the reason for his Indian name. In her next breath, she wondered about the name his parents gave him. Someday she'd ask.

As though he sensed her scrutiny, he swung his gaze from the fire to where she lay beneath the wagon. "You should be asleep." No compassion for the day. No sympathy in the plight of her parents.

"So should you."

"Tomorrow will be hard, and the days to come won't give you a reprieve."

"It's been that way since Independence," she said. "And I expect you're right about hard times with the wagon train leaving us behind." If he'd been Papa, she'd have scrambled from under the wagon to join him. They enjoyed long talks. "I'm sorry about today."

His hard stare sent her heart pounding, as though he hated her. "I made my choice."

She took a deep breath. "I suppose being married will change your plans."

"I won't let it. I've got important things to do."

"Is scouting your job?"

"Yes, but I'm heading to Oregon like the rest of 'em."

"What will you do there?"

"No more talk. I need time to think."

Sarah Jane gasped. His stinging response told fathoms of how he preferred a solitary life. Papa groaned and shifted above her, sending waves of guilt over her for attempting a brief reprieve. She rolled out from under the wagon. "You don't have to stay here," she said. "I can nurse Mama and Papa and later catch up with the other wagons. No point in you sitting here all miserable."

Painted Hands stood. He reminded her of a huge bear ready to pounce. "I keep my word. You'd die out here alone."

"I may die anyway." She'd not be bullied into thinking Painted Hands was her only chance of survival.

"That's right."

As soon as he hurled those words, she stepped to the rear of the wagon and climbed inside. If tonight gave any indication of how they'd get along for the rest of their married life, they'd most likely destroy each other.

Papa's ravings seized her attention. He called out for his ma, uttering childlike phrases. Sarah Jane touched his head. She jerked back her hand as alarm raced through her. *The lantern. I want to see his face.* In her haste to climb down, she caught her dress and fell backward. Her head hit the ground with a thud. For a moment, she lay there stunned, her head throbbing and her eyes flashing streaks of light. Strong arms lifted her from behind and righted her.

"Are you all right?" he asked without a trace of emotion.

She nodded slowly and remembered the urgency. "Papa's worse," she said. "I need to see him and get some tea down him."

"I'll tend to him." Painted Hands urged her to sit down with a gentleness that surprised her.

In the shadows, she glanced up into Painted Hands's face. He didn't look nearly as ominous.

"He's talking out of his mind." Sarah Jane closed her eyes in hopes of settling the pain searing the back of her head.

"Typhoid does that." He stood and lifted the lantern from the side of the wagon, then disappeared inside.

While she waited for him to return, she struggled with what to do for Papa, and she hadn't checked on Mama. Earlier Sarah Jane had worked hard in getting spoonfuls of tea down them and wiping their faces and necks with water. Nothing seemed to help.

God, please heal Mama and Papa. I've done all I can.

Sarah Jane braced herself with the side of the wagon and pulled herself to her feet. Her head spun, but after blinking several times, the dizziness faded. Holding on, she peered inside. Painted Hands blocked her view.

"Does he appear worse to you?" she asked.

"I'm afraid so. Your ma is unconscious, and she feels hotter."

She recalled Painted Hands's insistence on not wanting her to speak. Even so, she needed answers to her questions. "What can I do?"

"Wait and continue with what you've been doing." He eased back out of the wagon and stood beside her. "How's your head?"

"Better. What else can I expect?" She thought he might refuse to reply.

"Depends on each person. I'd say dysentery, more confusion, possibly a rash on the lower chest and stomach."

"How long will it all last?"

"Hard to tell, Sarah Jane. It could be days. It could be until morning." His voice sounded firm, and she wondered if he didn't think Mama and Papa would live.

"Do you think they're going to die?"

He leaned against the wagon. His relaxed stance took away from his Indian bearing. "Living and dying are not up to me. Your folks are real sick. They might pull through, and they might not."

"Mama's been poorly since we first started to Oregon. Leaving her friends behind made her sad." Sarah Jane pulled her shawl tighter around her shoulders. "The church women made her a friendship quilt just before we left. She loves that quilt, and I have it around her now."

"She needs to fight the fever. Tell her so even if you don't think she hears."

She sighed. "I'm afraid she'll give up. Papa has always been strong. Loved to work outside. Loved to play his fiddle. Loved talking to people. It's real hard seeing him. . .like this."

"Indian medicines would help, but I have none with me. I could ride out and look or search out the Indians in the area."

He hesitated. "But you'd be left alone, and I don't know how long I'd be gone."

"I have no idea what is best."

He rubbed the top of his hand as though trying to remove the scars. "I knew a man who believed in prayer. He said it changes a man from the inside out. I see you're a believer, and well, I think you need to hold onto your God."

"I've been praying until there are no more words."

"My friend said God hears our hearts."

"Are you a believer, too?"

He shook his head and pressed his lips together. "Kiowa believe in many spirits, not just one God like you. I reckon I'm more Kiowa than white."

Sarah Jane remembered Papa saying in order to reach folks with the gospel of Jesus Christ, a man must understand what the other person believes. "I hope one day you will tell me about those spirits."

"You make a strange comment for a Christian."

"I want to know what's important to you. I'm your wife now."

Immediately, Painted Hands stiffened. "I want you to understand the truth here. I never wanted a wife. I have important business in Oregon, matters that don't involve a woman or a family. Once we're there, I'll take care of undoing what Sanders insisted was proper."

A wisp of a breeze blew back her hair. To Sarah Jane, the wind felt like a touch of God, letting her know of His love and provision. A woman who lived wary of her husband might never be happy as God intended for married folk. "I'd like for us to be friends," she said.

"I'm a loner."

Papa used to say a man who didn't want friends had something to hide. "Maybe in the weeks to come you'll change your mind."

"Too many men have tried."

But they weren't your wife.

five

Sarah Jane prayed constantly for the strength and courage to withstand the hours and days to come. She feared for her stricken parents and the stranger who was now her husband. She no longer thought about taking a respite to sleep or eat; instead, she kept a vigil over Mama and Papa, doing all she could to keep them comfortable. At times, she talked to them. Her words moved from the hope and promise of the Northwest Territory, reminding them of the wondrous stories of rich earth and thick green forests, to the sweet memories left behind in Nebraska but alive in their hearts.

Painted Hands tended to cooking and making certain a plentiful supply of water was at hand. Camping beside the Platte River assured them they wouldn't run out. Sarah Jane and Painted Hands said little more than those things necessary in passing. She didn't have the stamina to encourage the friendship she deemed important, and she understood he preferred to be left alone. Later, when Mama and Papa were well, she'd concentrate on her husband. Odd that her new status took some getting used to, even if they were married in name only. For that concession, she thanked God. Outwardly, she refused to show signs of apprehension around Painted Hands. Inwardly she quivered at the thought of his touching her. Never one given to gossip, she repeatedly pushed the stories about him from her mind, but in dark moments, they haunted her.

A strange predicament, this marriage to a stranger. She recalled his offer to search out medicine from the prairie or from neighboring Indians. She appreciated his willingness to do whatever might help Mama and Papa, even if she'd be left alone. God was always her companion; yet she feared the dangers of predators both animal and human. In the past, Indians had viewed the wagon train from a distance or stopped to trade with the hundreds of sojourners. The Sioux were ferocious looking, and she prayed they never approached the lone wagon.

Sarah Jane held the distinction of a woman defenseless against those who could easily overpower her. What good would she do Mama and Papa if she were abducted by Indians? Unwelcome thoughts tramped miles of fears and insecurities. For certain, she didn't want Painted Hands to venture out for the medicine; neither did she want to be accused of being selfish. What if Mama and Papa died when the Indian remedies could have healed them?

Precious Father in heaven, help me discern Your will. I am so confused.

The Twenty-third Psalm, the verses often spoken over graves, broke into her ponderings.

"Yea, though I walk through the valley of the shadow of death, I will fear no evil; for Thou art with me; Thy rod and Thy staff they comfort me."

Tell me how not to be afraid, Father.

Trust, My daughter. My will is woven into your life.

In the darkness, Sarah Jane heard a rustle and turned to see Painted Hands at the rear of the wagon.

"How are they?" he asked.

She wiped her forehead, then focused on Mama and Papa. "I believe they're worse. The rash has thickened on their stomachs and the lower part of their chests." Swallowing the emotion threatening to overcome her, she took a deep breath and whispered, "Tell me what to do."

"Climb down and let me take a look." He held out his hand, and she took it. His touch felt strong and secure, and she needed something solid to hold onto.

Outside, she grabbed the coffeepot and filled a tin cup. The hot liquid tasted bitter, but it helped settle her fragile emotions.

She should ask Painted Hands to look for medicine in the morning. God promised never to leave her or forsake her. Her selfishness dare not steal the life from Mama and Papa.

Moments later, Painted Hands joined her at the fire. He poured coffee for himself and kicked at a cow chip, sending it into the smoldering fire. "Sarah Jane, I'm thinking you need to talk about your folks."

"Why is that?" She sensed the color drain from her face. The answer lay in the shadows of truth, a dark place where she refused to walk.

"Your ma and pa—they aren't going to live." Unlike the past, Painted Hands spoke with tenderness. "Their spirits are giving in to the typhoid."

"No." Sarah Jane covered her mouth to hide the weeping.

"You've done all you can. Be brave now." He paused and took her hand. "Let's talk."

She swiped at her eyes. Prayer. Yes, more prayer and God would heal Mama and Papa. God wanted her to trust Him—not the words of a heathen who refused to believe in God. "I must pray harder. God must not have heard me." She pulled back her hand and started toward the wagon, but Painted Hands swung her around to face him.

"Listen to me. There is nothing you can do. If you insist upon sitting with them, I'll go with you."

She longed to give in to the hysteria, but Mama and Papa needed her. Later, no matter what happened, she'd allow herself to feel the pain. Sarah Jane nodded. Inside the wagon, he held up the lantern. Gasping, she saw exactly what Painted Hands meant. Their shallow breathing and the gray pallor indicated the beginnings of death. But she would not give up until Mama and Papa breathed their last.

"Are you the only child?" Painted Hands asked.

Forcing back the weeping, she found the strength to answer Painted Hands's question. "The only living child. Two little girls died of summer complaint before I was born."

"You are their legacy."

Legacy? A strange word for Painted Hands. "I'd never thought of it that way."

"Their blood flows through your body. They will never really die but will live on in you and your children and your grandchildren."

She glanced at him curiously, yearning to hear more. His words, like rich poetry, took her mind off the inevitable.

"The seeds here in this wagon are for planting when you arrive in Oregon. Did they come from good plants?"

Sarah Jane nodded, and he continued. "Only at the end of harvest when the beauty and usefulness of a plant are gone can one gather seeds. The plant lives on in its seed to accomplish the same as the parent plant."

" 'I tell you the truth, unless a kernel of wheat falls to the ground and dies, it remains only a single seed. But if it dies, it produces many seeds.' " She recited the scripture as though it were a prayer.

Painted Hands smiled, the first she'd seen. "I've read the passage."

Yet, Painted Hands did not believe. The Kiowa gods had a firm grip on him, and she vowed to pray for his release.

"What you've told me makes this easier to bear." She studied Mama and Papa, touching one cheek, then the other and lingering on Mama's. "I understand, but life without them will be so hard."

"We are all dying from the moment life is breathed into us."

"Papa said our days on earth are to prepare us for the hereafter."

"Your father spoke with wisdom."

She twisted to see Painted Hands's face. "You, too, speak with wisdom. I wish I knew what to do while we wait. Prayer alone seems so feeble."

"You will honor them best by being strong. What is your pa's name?" he asked.

"John William, and Mama's name is Lydia Jane."

"And you are named after her."

"Mama and my grandmother Benson, Papa's mother."

"Where are you from?" Painted Hands leaned into the rear of the wagon. His voice echoed across the darkness as though he belonged with the night creatures.

"Near Lincoln, Nebraska. We lived in a sod house on a farm. Papa kept hearing about how he could get rich operating a mercantile in Independence where wagon trains left for out West. He couldn't resist, not with his adventurous streak. Mama didn't like the idea, but she finally agreed. Once we arrived in Independence, talk of Oregon got into his blood, and before long, he caught the fever, too." She took a deep breath at the utterance of the word *fever*.

"Go on," he urged.

"Then Papa abandoned the idea of purchasing a mercantile for the territory beyond the mountains. Not much more to tell. He signed on with Mr. Greenham's wagon train, and we purchased the provisions needed. Mama fretted over Papa's plans, but he believed we should go."

"Did you want to come?"

Sarah Jane tilted her head in remembrance. "Oh, I wanted to go, although the preparations were more work than I thought. I inherited Papa's desire to see and do new things."

"And now?" His words were barely above a whisper.

She touched a cloth to Papa's face while pondering the question. "I can't turn around and go back. If I gave up, I wouldn't be my father's child."

"And your ma? What are you going to carry on about her?"

Sarah Jane probed her mind in search of the special something she wanted to treasure about Mama. "Your questions make me think, but that's good. I need to have purpose and meaning in my life. Before Mama started feeling poorly, she used to laugh a lot. She looked for the good in folks and never tired in helping others. She enjoyed taking food to those who needed it or visiting the sick."

"Your life will be full, Sarah Jane."

She bit down hard on her lip to keep from breaking down into sobs. "I hope so." Sarah Jane's fingers caressed her mother's cheek. The skin felt hard, cooler. "Oh, no." She buried her face in her hands, no longer able to hide the unfathomable grief.

❧

Painted Hands thought Lydia Benson had died some moments before while Sarah Jane talked. He'd felt the woman's wrist for a steady beat and discovered none existed, but he hadn't wanted to interrupt. The memories of Sarah Jane's parents were more important than the precise moment of death. If he was not mistaken, Mr. Benson had passed away, too. He stepped down from the wagon to let her deal with the loss. He gripped the side of the wagon and watched, not sure what he should do.

Many new graves would lead the way to Oregon, all belonging to the wagons that had abandoned the Bensons. Typhoid. He'd seen it wipe out half a population, leaving widows and orphans to limp through life with only the memories of their loved ones to console them. He'd seen cholera and smallpox, too, but Painted Hands had escaped them and hoped to again. Now he wondered about Sarah Jane. His wife.

Her quiet weeping broke into his thoughts. Her shoulders rose and fell. He wrestled with comforting her, but he fought the intimacy it invited. A long time ago, he vowed never to feel the pain of losing loved ones again. If he attempted to console her, he risked growing close. If he grew close, he'd feel the agony of loss. Typhoid could attack Sarah Jane this very night. She could die in the next few days. Why allow himself to feel?

"Papa!"

He held his breath, certain Sarah Jane must have discovered her father no longer lived. He well remembered the terror of losing both parents at the same time.

The gruesome memories washed over him once more, bringing to the surface the cold night that a raging fire destroyed his family. The flames snatched up those he loved and left him to hear their screams forever. He'd done nothing to help until it was too late, and the scars on his hands were only futile reminders.

Releasing his hold on the wagon, Painted Hands made his way back to the fire. For Sarah Jane to find strength, she must toughen in this barren land. If he allowed her to depend on him, he'd delay the process. Once his obligation was fulfilled, she'd be on her own. This night marked the beginning of her training ground. Let her harden like the sun baking the ground around them. It had worked for him. Painted Hands stared up into the starlit night. A gnawing sensation bit at his stomach, a mixture of guilt and regret. The thought of Sarah Jane living years of misery as he had was cruel. Did he really want her to exist alone and fearful of love?

Painted Hands heard the Reverend Crandle's voice whispering around him. *You need to love, Painted Hands. Without it, we are nothing. For this commandment which I commanded thee this day, it is not hidden from thee, neither is it far off.*

Miles from the kindly man who showed him the mark of a true believer, Painted Hands still heard the lessons. He ran from the Reverend Crandle in search of answers to his miserable existence, away from the one man who had loved him even when Painted Hands fled from God. Reverend Crandle had been more than a father and a friend; but what he asked was too difficult, and his spirit cried out for release. Turning from the young woman who needed him in her hour of sorrow was wrong, but he couldn't comfort her. The past pain consumed him, the barrier around his heart too tall and too wide.

Sarah Jane's sobs roared in his ears, not the loudness of her cries, but the depths of despair. The teachings of Reverend Crandle urged him to go to her, and yet, he stayed affixed, silently begging her to cease. He poured another cup of coffee and allowed his wretched soul to feed his tortured mind. A raw part of him remembered the little boy who pulled the charred remains of his sister from the burning home. The sound of his own wails had been heard by a Kiowa hunting party.

At last, Sarah Jane's weeping stopped. He breathed relief and wiped perspiration streaming down his face—certainly not a factor from the chilly night air but the result of tremors from his past. He faced the wagon. Preparing the bodies for burial was a task he could accomplish. A breeze caught the canvas flap and whisked it back and forth as though the spirits of Mr. and Mrs. Benson escaped from their beds.

"Sarah Jane," he called. "Are you all right?"

In the next instant, she climbed down from the wagon. Even in the shadows, he could see her tear-stained face and swollen eyes. "I'm not all right, but I'm sure God in His mercy will make each moment a little easier to bear."

"I'm sorry."

She half-nodded. "They are in the arms of Jesus."

The words sounded as though they were memorized and appropriate rather than how she honestly felt.

"I'll prepare them and dig the holes for burial."

She hugged the shawl to her shoulders and ventured closer to the dying fire. "I can help."

"I think you should sleep, and there is only one shovel."

"Sleep will evade me, I'm sure."

"Then consider what you want to say over your parents in the morning."

She nodded, then shivered. "I do regret that your kind heart has been repaid with these dire circumstances."

"There is nothing kind about me, Sarah Jane. But what of you?"

She sighed, her thin shoulders shaking. "I will live for the legacy you spoke of. Without your wisdom, I'd die this very night. God bless you, Painted Hands, for allowing our Father to use you in my hour of distress."

six

Sarah Jane woke the following morning with tears dried on her cheeks and feeling very much alone. She'd fallen asleep begging God for an answer to why her parents were taken. Now she felt guilty for sleeping when a needling voice told her she should stay awake and record all of the pleasant memories about her parents into Mama's journal. Did God think she didn't love them enough—that she was a selfish daughter who fell asleep on the eve of their funeral?

Today the remains of Mama and Papa would be laid to rest in an earthen hole. Their spirits had fled their sickened bodies and now waited with the Lord until she joined them. Sarah Jane didn't know how she'd go on. The sound of Mama's musical laughter would linger with her always. Back in Nebraska, ladies from all around came to quilt with Mama. Her perfect stitching and the way she pieced pattern sections into unique designs made Sarah Jane and Papa proud, but Mama never took the credit. She said God guided her needle. Papa's wisdom helped Sarah Jane understand the scriptures and how to apply them to her life. Their days had been good in Nebraska despite the blizzards in winter, the twisters in summer, and the unpredictable weather during planting and harvesting. But they had all been happy.

As much as she treasured Papa, he must not have heard God's direction in the journey to Oregon.

A part of Sarah Jane would always dwell in the past, where she felt secure and loved. Now she faced an uncertain future with Painted Hands. She had a husband; she was a wife, but she did not possess a real marriage. At the moment, she appreciated his not insisting she take a wifely role. Once they reached

Oregon, he'd make the arrangements to dissolve the marriage. As much as she understood their union was in name only, the thought of not being fit for him made her feel worthless. She wasn't the plainest woman on the wagon train; maybe he had his eye on someone else. Sarah Jane remembered the scriptures said the man was the head of the household, so he must know best about going their own way in Oregon.

What is wrong with me? Here I am pondering over Painted Hands's displeasure with me on the morning of Mama and Papa's funeral.

In the way lay all the things Mama and Papa needed to begin homesteading and later open a mercantile. The daunting task frightened her, for she knew little about cultivating the land and even less about operating a business. In the trunk, Papa had made notes about both endeavors. She needed to find the written instruction and study it at nights.

"God has equipped us for this world," Papa had said. "We look to Him for direction, and He guides our paths."

"I'll not disappoint you," she whispered. "I'll simply look for God's messenger to light my way."

Glancing about, Sarah Jane wondered where Painted Hands had gone. She rolled from underneath the wagon and stood. The smell of coffee brought her to the present. Her mental despair had masked the otherwise enticing smell. He must have brewed it earlier, but where could he be? She turned her attention to the rear of the wagon. He could be digging the graves—a job in which she should help, although Papa had but one shovel. *Breakfast.* She must prepare a good meal for Painted Hands. She needed the bacon and flour stored inside the wagon, beside Mama and Papa. That meant seeing them again—lifeless. Eating did not appeal to her, but she had a duty to her husband.

Another thought clutched her heart. What if he had ridden off? Left her to fend for herself?

Terror twisted up her spine. She hurried to the opposite

side of the wagon and saw his horse grazing on a single tuft of grass. Releasing a heavy sigh, she willed the queasy sensation in the pit of her stomach to vanish. Too many things must be done, whether she felt ill or well. Moving back to the fire, she poured a cup of coffee, then stared in an easterly direction. Painted Hands bent over, digging into the hard earth. A shovel of dirt, then another dumped onto a heap beside him. Obviously, he'd been working for some time. Guilt assaulted her again for sleeping while he labored on the hard prairie.

Last night she needed him to offer her comfort. He chose to let her grieve in privacy. When they were on the trail again, she'd ask him if the Kiowa mourned the dead alone. Another thought occurred to her. Mama's and Papa's deaths could remind him of his family's tragic deaths.

He had urged her to talk and remember, but oh, how she craved the arms of another human being. Perhaps she was weak. Shaking her head to dispel the nagging thought of the undesirable trait, she elected to take him a canteen of water at the gravesite. She didn't want to look at Mama and Papa; rather, she preferred to see them in her mind where they were happy and whole.

Sarah Jane moved slowly, not sure what to say or how to help. The barbaric stories told about Painted Hands crept through her mind; yet she believed they were false. Her husband had been raised by Indians, and he preferred their ways; that made him an oddity. Folks tended to criticize what they didn't know or understand—another one of Papa's sayings. Or was she attempting to convince herself? Papa had warned her about Painted Hands. Why? Did he simply not know the man and fell prey to the consensus of most of the other folks on the wagon train? She hoped so; she prayed so.

Painted Hands glanced up when she arrived. She handed him the canteen, and he thanked her with a nod. Sweat dotted his brow with a trickle down the side of his face. If not for the beads woven in his hair, he'd look like a mountain man. When she gathered her wits to see the burial holes, she saw only one, and it was being widened to hold a second body.

"Good morning," she said, studying his face. "How early did you rise?"

He leaned on the shovel and released a labored sigh. "I didn't go to bed."

Stunned, she grasped for words. "You shouldn't have done all this alone. I could have helped."

"Sarah Jane, you were exhausted from caring for your folks. With only one shovel, what would you have done?"

She shrugged. "Kept you in coffee? Let you rest while I dug awhile?"

He stepped on the shovel and lifted another heap of dirt. "I am hungry."

"I can prepare food. I'll tend to it right away."

Silence separated them, as it had before. She'd have to climb into the wagon for the food—and see Mama and Papa.

"Thank you for all you've done. I'll have breakfast ready shortly." Sarah Jane turned to leave.

"I've covered your parents' bodies. There's no need for you to look at them."

She stopped and whirled around. He knew her thoughts. "Truly you are a gift from God."

Painted Hands continued at his work. Without lifting his head, he appeared to speak his words to the empty grave. "I think not."

"You have been ever so kind."

"You've heard the tales. Don't tell me you haven't." He thrust the shovel into the hard ground with such force that she sucked in a breath.

She crossed her arms over her chest. "Are you saying they are true?"

He peered up at her, his emotionless face offering no indication of the man inside. "You should be frightened."

Anger rose within Sarah Jane. "Frightened? My parents are dead. I have no choice but to move on to Oregon. The wagon train is surely plagued with typhoid victims, which tells me Mama and Papa will always be blamed because they were the first to be ill. My husband can't wait to be rid of me." With each word, she spat fury and grief. Selfishness clouded her thinking, but at the moment she didn't care. "I thank you for what you've done, then you bully me? What is left for me to fear? Ridicule? Abandonment? Disease? Death?" She clamped her lips together before tossing another word. Lifting her chin, she started back to the wagon. "Your breakfast will take but a short while."

"Sarah Jane."

She had no intentions of letting him see her weep and marched ahead. "I owe you an apology, but not now—later."

"Would you rather bury them before eating? The sun will be hot before long."

The familiar lump rose in her throat. She blinked several times before responding. "Yes, please."

"I'm nearly finished here. I suggest you retrieve your Bible from the wagon before I return for your folks."

She paused to gain control. "I've been thinking about that very thing." She kept on walking, despising herself for not apologizing for her outburst and believing Painted Hands deserved her wrath in the same breath.

His mannerisms, so cold and unfeeling, swept over her like a wintry chill. Did the man have no compassion? Was this the Indian part of him? If so, they were truly barbaric and heathen. No wonder women clutched their children to their breast and men reached for their shotguns at the mention of Indians. The fear of hostiles murdering and torturing their captives made sense. Horrible, perfect sense.

She didn't need Painted Hands for sympathy. His backbreaking work would suffice, and once they caught up to the wagon train—providing they were permitted—he could go back to scouting for Mr. Greenham and she'd take care of herself.

He's your husband. You made a promise to God.

She held her breath. Must she be reminded? After all, it hadn't been consummated.

You promised God to bind yourself to this man until death.

Maybe she'd contract typhoid and die like Mama and Papa. The grave would solve everything. Maybe she'd pray for that very thing.

Are you a child or a woman?

The voice of the One who ruled the universe would not release her. *Why, God? I don't understand. Do You despise me? Is that why my life has fallen to the depths? Do You even care?* Always the questions and no answers. Papa always quoted scripture when folks didn't understand adversity. She could hear his booming voice still. " 'And we know that all things work together for good to them that love God, to them who are the called according to His purpose.' "

What was the purpose of loving God if He chose to destroy everything she held dear? How could any good come of this? *Just tell me, Lord. I see nothing ahead but more heartache.*

Her body numb and her heart broken, Sarah Jane trudged ahead until she reached the rear of the wagon. Paralyzed, she simply couldn't bring herself to fetch the Bible. Upon peering inside, she saw Painted Hands had covered the bodies with Mama's friendship quilt. The embroidered words *Remember me* seemed to lift off the coverlet and wrap its message around her heart. Mama and Papa were no longer there but in heaven. But touching them in order to fetch Papa's Bible made her cringe.

"I'll get the Book for you," Painted Hands said.

She hadn't heard him approach. Indians were silent, so Papa had said. They learned to walk without making a sound. Sarah Jane stepped aside and made her way back to the fire. "It's inside the trunk, on the top."

She listened to the creak of the lid's hinge, realizing he'd unfastened the leather straps. A moment later, he handed her the Bible.

"I can read, if it's too difficult for you." His voice sounded gentle.

Rubbing her fingers over the rough grain of the cover, she wanted to cry again. Painted Hands did have a tad of decency. She turned her attention to the site of her parents' final resting place. "Papa's favorite passage was Psalm One. Mama had several."

"The man I lived with after the soldiers took me from the Kiowa used to read Psalm Twenty-three at funerals. He thought the passage befited those who were grieving."

"Can we read both?"

"Yes, ma'am."

Sarah Jane tore her gaze from the graves to his face. To her comfort, she saw a touch of compassion in his blue eyes. "Thank you."

"You will be able to endure this day, Sarah Jane. You're a strong woman."

She shrugged. "I feel like the crumbled dirt beneath our feet."

"Dirt packed together is what forms the earth. Come—let's get this thing done."

She agreed with him on that matter. "What shall I do?" she asked.

Painted Hands pointed to the fire. "Sit and wait for me. I'm going to hitch up the oxen and take your parents to their graves. Then I'll call for you."

She glanced at the smoldering chips, then back to him. "Seems like I need to do something more."

"You loved and nursed them while they were alive. I'll do what I can for them in death."

His simple words made sense; she nodded her compliance.

"I do know the sadness in your heart," Painted Hands said. "My family still lives inside me, and I see their faces lit with joy."

"How old were you?"

"Six. I thought for many years that I was the only survivor, but the Reverend Crandle learned of an older brother. He lives in Oregon."

"That is why you're with the wagon train," she said. If he'd have mentioned this part of his life before, she wouldn't have been so quick to criticize.

"Scouting kept me separated from the other folks who don't care for my ways." He repositioned his hat.

"I'm sure they'll feel differently since we're married and you helped me with Mama and Papa."

"I'm still the same man." The coldness whispered through his reply. "Typhoid has probably spread through the rest of them by now."

"Should we travel alone?" She braced herself, knowing how he preferred solitude.

"I could make it fine, but it would be lonesome for you." He headed toward the oxen.

Taking Papa's Bible, she opened it to the worn pages where he'd penned his thoughts or written dates that meant nothing to her. Again she asked to see God's power in this. Only silence, the dreadful finality of silence.

While she busied herself around the fire, Painted Hands wrapped Mama in the friendship quilt and Papa in another, then tied their bodies with rope and lifted them back into the wagon.

"I'll call for you after I lower them."

He drove away, leaving her more alone than she could ever remember. Bile rose in her throat, and she thought for certain she'd be ill. A short while later, Painted Hands called for her. At the gravesite, he read Psalms One and Twenty-three, then a passage from First Corinthians, chapter fifteen.

" 'In a moment, in the twinkling of an eye, at the last trump: for the trumpet shall sound, and the dead shall be raised incorruptible, and we shall be changed.' "

Sarah Jane listened to every word as he continued to read.

" 'O death, where is thy sting? O grave, where is thy victory?' "

God spoke to her in those words. Her rebellious stand against God shamed her. *Please forgive me, Father. I know Mama and Papa are with You. My tears are for myself.* How strange that God should choose to speak His words through a man who did not trust in Him. Maybe Painted Hands did believe but had chosen to run.

" 'Therefore, my beloved brethren, be ye steadfast, unmoveable, always abounding in the work of the Lord, forasmuch as ye know that your labour is not in vain in the Lord.' "

I will, Father. I will not forget my marriage vows or the lessons Mama and Papa taught me.

seven

Painted Hands pounded dirt into the graves by repeatedly running the wagon wheels over the final resting place of John and Lydia Benson. The procedure deterred animals from digging up the bodies for food and some unscrupulous folks—both white man and Indian—from stealing their clothes. Once he finished, he needed to talk to Sarah Jane about breaking camp and catching up with the wagon train.

He avoided the stares and barbs aimed in his direction and enjoyed the solitude away from the people. Those who singled him out were more heathen than any Kiowa he ever knew. If an Indian brother despised you, you understood the reason why, and you could choose an opportunity to prove yourself worthy. Among too many white people, the judgment was made without considering the heart of a man. Not all whites were this way but far too many, just as some Kiowa did not represent their race well.

The Reverend Crandle honored every man through his faith. He'd shown Painted Hands kindness and lived his teachings in the respect and dignity shown to others. The reverend's manner of life had led the way for many folks to want to live like him. Sarah Jane also modeled integrity. Her honesty and willingness to extend herself unselfishly had affected Painted Hands. She'd touched him more than he cared to admit. He had yet to understand why her presence bristled and warmed him at the same time.

Yesterday and today he wanted to comfort her, but physically placing his arms around her grieving body and allowing her to weep against his chest battled against his vow to keep people away. When he closed his eyes at night, he saw

Sarah Jane's face and lived the longing to protect her against those forces that threatened to hurt or sadden her. How many times had he lost himself in those green eyes? She had a beauty about her that rivaled nature. Her reddish-blond hair and matching freckles projected youth and a glimpse of honey sweetness, but Sarah Jane's true loveliness came from within. If he didn't keep a shield over his emotions, she'd melt his resolve to let nothing stand in the way of reaching Jacob.

He vaguely remembered his older brother. At the time of the fire, Jacob already worked with their pa on the farm and did most of the milking. Painted Hands looked up to him, but the older boy didn't have much need for a younger brother tagging along behind. Painted Hands quickly earned the nickname "Puppy." What a nuisance he'd been, crying to Ma when Jacob shooed him away like a pesky fly. Those distant memories brought a smile to his lips. Once he found Jacob, he hoped the two of them could find the time to establish a lost relationship.

He stole a look at Sarah Jane. She bent to turn a slab of sizzling bacon in the frying pan. She had the faith he wished he'd succumbed to. Reverend Crandle had shown him the way, and Painted Hands even prayed for forgiveness and a new life in Jesus Christ, but that was before.

Nightmarish recollections stole the joy wanting to break through his rough exterior. The same day Painted Hands realized he needed God to lead and direct his life, various townsfolk visited Reverend Crandle with a false accusation about Painted Hands murdering a family outside town. The sheriff arrested him with no more proof than his Indian style of clothes and the way he wore his hair. Reverend Crandle and his wife prayed continuously. The law found the killer, but in the meantime, gossip about Reverend Crandle housing a murderer spread through the town. The church asked the reverend to resign. That's when Painted Hands decided he wanted no part of the Christian faith. He turned from God with a vow never to return.

"Don't let the weakness of man destroy your faith," the reverend had said. "All believers are saints who sin."

"I can't have faith in a God who allows unjust punishment," Painted Hands said.

"What of Jesus? Remember His death?"

Painted Hands shook his head. "I don't know. I think God will have to show me His power, because all I see is evil."

That had happened over seven years ago. Painted Hands continued to live with the Reverend Crandle awhile longer to try to sort out his future. Then he elected to join up with Greenham's wagon train as a scout. Painted Hands already had the skills, and Greenham gave him direction. Then some months ago came the unexpected. Painted Hands never tired of recalling every word.

"I have good news for you," the reverend had said. "I've located your brother, Jacob."

Painted Hands at last sensed hope. "Are you sure?"

The man grinned. "I'm certain. He listed parents Timothy and Elizabeth Carlson as perished in a fire along with three sisters: Rose Alice, Leah Mae, and Mary Elizabeth. He also named a deceased brother, Toby William. They were all from near Council Bluffs along the Missouri River."

"Where is Jacob?" Painted Hands could barely contain his excitement. Pictures of the older brother flashed through his memories.

"He left about ten months ago for Oregon. His friends stated he planned to start a logging camp north of the Willamette Valley."

"I have to find him." Painted Hands laughed. "My brother is alive."

"And it's an answer to prayer," Reverend Crandle said. "God's hand is in this. I can feel His presence."

Painted Hands didn't want to attribute the good news to

God, but he sensed an exhilaration in his whole body. Not a single day since then had the desire wavered to reunite with Jacob. If he could have climbed on the wings of an eagle, he'd have flown to Oregon, but one obstacle after another lengthened the miles between them. The reverend stated the journey to the Northwest meant a fresh start—one without malicious tongues. On this last trip to Oregon, Painted Hands wanted to make friends among the travelers, except someone already knew the old stories and spread them through the camp faster than a prairie fire. He hoped things would be different when he reached his brother.

Once more, Painted Hands knew the pain of isolation. This time he'd learned his lesson. No one would venture close; no one but Jacob, although his brother might shun him.

Shaking aside the thoughts that repeated in his head, Painted Hands moved his ponderings to the present.

"We need to decide about what to do next," he said after he'd unhitched the oxen and the two ate their meal.

She lifted her gaze; a curly wisp of reddish-blond hair trailed down the side of her face. Innocence and a sense of trust greeted him. He must be strong and fight his growing feelings.

"I think joining back up with the wagon train makes good sense."

"You mean if they will have us," she said.

"Don't think on it that way. If they are dying of typhoid, we don't want them, either."

She nodded. "But they treated you shamefully."

"I'm used to it."

"I still want to go to Oregon."

A wolf howled in the distance and grasped his attention. He waited for another one, but it never came. Hostile Indians sometimes spoke to each other through bird and animal calls. "My plans haven't changed."

She tilted her head and looked about. "There's nothing keeping us here. When do you want to leave?"

"As soon as we can get started." He searched her face for signs of remorse; when her placid features revealed nothing, he finished his bacon and biscuits. "Can we leave in an hour?"

❧

At the designated time, Sarah Jane climbed onto the wagon seat, and Painted Hands rode alongside. Papa's horse was tied to the rear of the wagon. Mama and Papa lay behind them without so much as a wooden box to cradle their bodies. The stretch of road ahead provided time to think and plan. In the bottom of the trunk, hidden in the folds of one of Mama's dresses, was money to purchase land in Oregon and the beginnings of a mercantile. She considered selling Papa's horse and saddle at Fort Laramie and hiding the money, too.

Her gaze swung to Painted Hands. This should be a matter she discussed with her husband—if he were a real husband. Since he chose a loveless existence, then she'd keep financial matters to herself. What would stop him from taking the money, leaving her penniless? If only they were friends, like Mama and Papa used to be. Her parents often talked way into the night, never running out of topics. Sarah Jane wanted to learn about Painted Hands—his life with the Kiowa, their customs and language.

Painted Hands preferred not to talk. He'd told her so. Wishing for a friend in him was futile at best, and she wasted her efforts and continuously faced disappointment every time she tried. Slapping the reins over the backs of the oxen, she chose to dwell on life once she got to Oregon. Operating a mercantile assured her of wonderful friends. Just thinking about the goods she'd carry and the customers she'd assist made her tingle. Bolts of beautiful cloth, bonnets, food, tools for the men, and jars of penny candy would line the shelves. She'd need a clever name for the store, maybe Sarah Jane's Supplies or Benson's Mercantile.

A realization seized her. She couldn't open a Benson's Mercantile; her name was. . .Mrs. Painted Hands. Peering at her husband, she decided to ask him.

"What do I tell folks my name is?"

He said nothing, and she wondered if he'd heard her. She opened her mouth to speak again, then he rode closer.

"My name?"

She nodded. "Yes. When folks ask me."

"I suppose my white-man name."

"Which is?"

"Toby Carlson."

Sarah Jane had learned something about her husband. *Sarah Jane Carlson.* She rolled the name on her tongue. It went together nicely—for as long as she was his wife. And he had a first name, too—Toby. "That's a good name."

"I don't imagine you'll have much of a chance to use it since I intend to get a divorce as soon as we get to Oregon. Might be best if you continue using your pa's name."

She didn't respond. What could she say? But the anger grew. Was she simply the wrong race? Maybe he didn't like the color of her hair or her freckles. She wasn't happy with her looks, either, especially the unruly curls. Her eyes—yes, that must be the problem. She knew she looked like a cat, but those things weren't supposed to matter. Mama said beauty had to come from the inside. She said comely people one day grew old, but the important traits only got better— the things you learned by living life and honoring God. How would Painted Hands ever see anything worthwhile in her when he kept his distance as though she embarrassed him?

Startled, she threw a seething look his way. He could use a shave and a haircut. Of course, he might be so ugly that everyone would run.

"Are you ashamed of me?" She hadn't intended to blurt out the question. It simply fell from her mouth.

"What are you talking about?" The deep tone of his voice fueled her fury. The sound by no means frightened her, especially when rage simmered near the surface.

"I understand you married me because of the committee. I

understand you're a humble man to help me take care of Mama and Papa, and I'm grateful. I understand we don't know each other, but I'm not *that* ugly."

Painted Hands adjusted his hat. "What are you talking about? Are you sick?"

"No, I'm not sick. I'm asking you what's wrong with me."

He stared straight ahead as if she'd gone mad. "I'm riding ahead for a camping site."

"Of course. Put miles between us as if there aren't enough right now. While you're out there scouting around, see if you can find a watering hole where I can take a bath."

He pressed his heels into the horse's side. "Yes, ma'am. I'll do my best."

The man didn't even have the sense to participate in an argument.

"Go ahead and be by yourself," she called after him.

The moment his figure faded, Sarah Jane regretted her childish temper tantrum. This wasn't like her. She always held her tongue and looked to the bright side of things. What if he kept right on riding? Everything he owned was stuffed in his saddlebag, except the provisions in the wagon. Why should he stay? Those Indian customs would keep him alive all the way to Oregon.

Sarah Jane's mind raced with how she might do the same thing. If the committeemen said she couldn't come back, then she'd find her way to Fort Laramie. There she'd join the next wagon train that rolled through. She wasn't a man, but she certainly had the means to look out for herself.

The afternoon wore on, the sun hotter than she could remember, and still no sign of Painted Hands. He really had left her. The sound of creaking wagon wheels scraped at her scrambled thoughts. A pair of buzzards flew overhead, creating a wave of uneasiness in the pit of her stomach. She watched the flight to make certain the vultures didn't head back toward Mama and Papa's grave.

They could be feasting on me in a few days. Forcing the gruesome image from her mind, she shielded her eyes in hopes of seeing Painted Hands. Nothing rose in her view but miles and miles of sparse grass beaten down by the cattle moving with the wagon train ahead.

"We'll catch up to Mr. Greenham's wagons," she said to the oxen. "They won't refuse me. After all, I didn't get the typhoid."

The echo of her voice proved how easily it would be to lose her mind in this desolate country. Now she understood Mama's desperation. All her mother had heard was the loneliness and nothing of the promise.

Isn't that what you're doing?

Sarah Jane swung her head from side to side looking for the source of the voice. So real, so clear. The silence repeated, and she shrugged.

What good is a promise without trust?

Did God think Mama didn't trust Him? She was one of the most faithful of all the believers Sarah Jane had ever seen.

You, My child. Where is your faith? Where is your trust?

She wanted desperately to have those things, but all she could see came in the form of Mama and Papa's grave and a husband who didn't want her.

Painted Hands is a good man.

How would she ever know? He despised her.

He is a child astray.

"What can I do?" she whispered.

Trust Me for the promises. Loneliness is for those in darkness.

Sarah Jane repeated the words she recognized as from the Father. Lately, she'd been incredibly selfish—fretting over things about herself instead of trusting God. He had a plan for her and for Painted Hands. The mysterious future was laid out by God like a huge feast waiting to be tasted. She craved joy in the engulfing sorrow. She pleaded for direction in the way of her husband and courage to complete the road to Oregon. Undoubtedly, obedience to God's directives proved more difficult than she ever imagined. *Loneliness is for those in darkness.*

Sarah Jane snuffed back a sob.

Forgive me for my faithless heart. I'll apologize to Painted Hands, and I promise to be a good wife—no matter what happens.

Her gaze lifted, and she saw a lone rider. Painted Hands had not deserted her. If not for fear of driving him even farther away, she'd have jumped from the wagon and run to him. Asking his forgiveness for her wild tongue meant humbling herself and possibly facing his rejection. From now on, she'd look at Painted Hands as Jesus saw him—totally loved and cherished.

The closer he rode, the more anxious she became. Once again, loneliness and insecurity washed over her, but she had not been abandoned. God had His hands on her shoulder, gently guiding her.

"Hello." She waved and forced a smile. "I am so sorry, Painted Hands, for the mean things I said. Will you forgive me?"

"No." He spit his words at her like an angry rattler. "The wagon train is not far ahead. From the tracks I see, maybe three days beyond us. I'll take you there; then I'm riding on."

eight

Painted Hands hated the way he treated Sarah Jane. She'd apologized to him and even smiled when he rode her way. Still, he had little choice. What kind of life did he have to offer? He'd become set in his ways—probably as mean as most folks liked to think. Best he lived a life of solitude. Everywhere he went, every person he learned to care about met with disaster: his family, the Kiowa, the Reverend Crandle, and now Sarah Jane. In an isolated part of his mind, he wondered if the Bensons would have lived if he'd not stepped up to help. God had cursed him and anyone who drew close. As much as he wanted to see Jacob, he questioned the wisdom of exposing his brother to the inevitable.

An unquenchable thirst to put miles between him and Sarah Jane consumed him. She pressed against his heart, more so than any other person ever had. He wanted to know her, open his scars that seemed to fester with age, and pray, really pray, for healing. But he dare not—the reminders of what always happened were as evident as his discolored hands. Reverend Crandle said Painted Hands bore the fire-bitten scars like a breastplate, a shield against freeing himself from pain.

Nothing could shake his determination as far as Sarah Jane was concerned. Every time he looked at her, his heart weakened. He must take action fast before he gave in and something happened to her. For too many years, he'd told himself he didn't need anyone. Most days he'd believed it, but with Sarah Jane, his heart wrenched for a love that would not let him go. He sensed a weakening of his will, no matter how hard he tried to disguise it.

Late afternoon they camped by the Platte River, where water

was shallow and plentiful. The cattle drank their fill, and with the approaching sunset, the picturesque scene swelled in his chest. How he would have loved to take his wife by the hand and watch the sunset together. The talk he claimed he didn't want would happen naturally. They could make plans for the future—discuss their ambitions about what lay ahead at the end of their journey. He had never asked what she wanted to do upon reaching the Northwest, if friends or relatives awaited her arrival or if she were alone. As for him, he hoped things went well with Jacob, and there might even be a job for him at the logging camp.

Fool! What is wrong with you? You have no choice but a solitary life. You destroy everything you touch.

Shaken back to reality, Painted Hands rode ahead to scout out more of the trail. Sarah Jane had indicated she wanted a bath. A fitting man would disappear into the gathering dusk and give her privacy. Releasing a heavy sigh, he decided that, by traveling on Sunday, they'd reach the wagon train in the allotted three days.

He'd seen the fresh graves, and by the number of them, typhoid had spread through the wagon train. The vengeful side of him claimed those folks had gotten their due, but the side of him that Reverend Crandle had touched felt sympathy for those who had lost loved ones. Which side of him was the real Toby Carlson, or would he eventually resign completely to Painted Hands—the half-crazed man who favored neither Indian nor white?

When darkness nearly enveloped him, he returned to the wagon. He stayed gone longer than he intended, but this way, she would be ready for bed once they ate.

The smell of frying fish assaulted his senses. His stomach growled. She'd gone fishing, and he knew without dwelling on it further that she'd done it for him. By this time, he realized a lot about Sarah Jane, and her giving heart didn't seem to end. The realization made him feel like a snake—a rattler at best.

"I have food ready," she said when he entered the firelight.

I have to enjoy this while I can. The days without Sarah Jane would be long.

Another smell tugged at him—fresh biscuits and the scent of apples. How warm it felt to have a woman tending to him.

"You didn't have to go to this much trouble." Painted Hands masked the feelings ready to burst through his crusty exterior.

"I wanted to." Her sweet voice reverberated over the night air. She heaped a tin plate full of fish, biscuits, and warm apples and handed it to him. Next she poured a steaming cup of hot coffee and set it beside him on the ground.

They ate in the typical silence he'd demanded from the beginning, but it wasn't what he truly wanted. He finished his food and asked for more.

"Must we separate when we catch up to the wagon train?" she asked.

The food suddenly caught in his throat. "We aren't suited for each other."

"I don't know you very well, but I want to. I can change if you tell me what makes you comfortable—"

"Being alone. No one else around." He dare not look at her for fear he'd forego his willpower at the sight of her angelic face.

"I would do whatever you ask."

"Why?" Painted Hands asked. "Is it your faith? Are you afraid of being alone for the rest of the journey? Is it the divorce?"

Her thin shoulders lifted and fell. "I'd be a liar if I said I wasn't afraid or that I didn't mind solitude. I'm not as strong as you. But I made a promise to God to submit as your wife. I'm asking for a chance to fulfill my vow."

Frustrated at her, frustrated at himself, he squeezed the handle on his mug. "Marriage will never work between us, Sarah Jane. There's no point in discussing it any longer or ever again." Gritting his teeth, he set the plate and mug down and stomped away in the dark.

For the first time in years, tears trickled down his cheeks.

❧

Sarah Jane had seen the graves, more than she ever hoped to see again. Some held stones as markers, others crude crosses, and too many appeared to be mass burials. Always wheels had firmed the dirt heaped overtop, and always she wondered who had fallen prey to the typhoid. A risk needled at her. By returning to the wagon train, she faced the possibility of getting the disease, too. With Painted Hands leaving, she had to endure whatever God saw fit.

Up ahead, speckles of cattle moved across the prairie. They'd caught up with Mr. Greenham.

"Painted Hands," she said, for he'd ridden his spotted horse beside her. "Would you please stay three days with me? I know you're set to go, but I'm begging."

He stared straight ahead. Long moments lingered in the quiet. No matter what he said, she'd not resort to tears.

"I can do that," he finally said.

Thank You, God. A smile tugged at her mouth. "I'll not be a burden to you. I need to talk to some folks about helping me on to Oregon, and the three days would give me time."

"You've never been trouble." He rode ahead then, always running from her as if she were distasteful.

You can't run forever, Painted Hands. Someday God will turn your heart back to Him.

As the wagon eased closer to the others, Painted Hands and Mr. Greenham rode to her. Their faces wore a grim expression. The news must not be good.

"Good afternoon," Mr. Greenham said, leaning on his saddle. "Sorry to hear about your parents."

Sarah Jane studied the lines on his face, more lines than she'd seen before. "How have you fared?"

"We lost lots of folks to the typhoid. Still have many folks down with it. The sickness spread the very night the committee voted you out."

That's why she and Painted Hands had caught up with the

wagons so quickly. "Are the Robinsons all right?" She couldn't bear to think of Martha and Amelia fretting with fever.

"We lost all of 'em," Mr. Greenham replied. "Buried them in a mass grave."

Sarah Jane shuddered. Several moments went by before she regained her composure. "The girls were my dearest friends, and my parents often visited Mr. and Mrs. Robinson. I do hope they didn't suffer much."

Mr. Greenham nodded. "So many have passed on that I don't remember all the particulars. No new cases yesterday or today," he said. "Thank God, it must be over."

"I'll pray for all of them." Sarah Jane understood the bereavement of those families. "Perhaps I can help in the nursing."

"You're a mighty kind woman to offer help. I won't be refusing you and Painted Hands to join up with us again, although I wonder the good sense of it."

"Traveling alone is dangerous," Painted Hands said. "I want my wife to have the protection you offer."

"You're a wise man. This country hollows out enough graves without increasing the chances." Mr. Greenham straightened in the saddle. "Go ahead and drive your cattle back into the herd and pull the wagon to the end of the line. As you can see, we haven't been making good time with so many down sick."

"Fort Laramie isn't far ahead," Painted Hands said. "Will they let us in?"

"Doubt it," Mr. Greenham said. "That will disappoint a lot of folks. The healthy ones most likely can get us supplies, and we'll rest up a few days." He turned his horse back toward the wagons. "I've missed you, Painted Hands. Glad you're back."

A few days ago, Sarah Jane would have fought the urge to encourage her husband to stay longer than the three days, but not now. An unexplainable peace wrapped around her insecurities with a message of comfort. God's way was the best.

That evening, Painted Hands left her without a word. She'd grown used to his disappearances. Would he give her a final good-bye at the end of the three days? She doubted he'd even considered a proper farewell. Avoidance best described her husband.

A cook fire warmed apples from the previous evening along with fried bacon and a few precious potatoes. She hoped Painted Hands arrived soon, for the day had been particularly taxing, and she craved sleep. All day her head hurt, and no wonder with the burden bearing down on her. After straightening the inside of the wagon and filling the water keg, she opened the trunk to seek out the money Papa had for Oregon. Resting the lantern on a sack of flour, she carefully pulled the bills from Mama's dress. To her amazement, the money amounted to over twice what Sarah Jane believed was hidden. She could open a mercantile right away. A note wrapped another bundle of money. She opened it and recognized the handwriting.

My beloved daughter,

If you are reading this, no doubt your papa and I perished along the journey to Oregon. I am sorry for abandoning you. Your papa and I prayed that God in His infinite wisdom would send someone to help you in the event of our deaths. Do not turn back. I know I protested leaving Nebraska, but your papa's dreams are far more important. Only you can fulfill his vision.

The amount of money here is far more than we told you. We wanted to keep a good portion for you in the event you married. Praise God there is plenty here for you to establish yourself in a new home.

My reason for this letter is to tell you how very much you are loved. The days and months ahead will be difficult, but I have no doubt you will see Oregon, the promised land, and it will be as beautiful as we dreamed.

Select your husband wisely. You have the means to take care of yourself, so a marriage out of necessity should not befall you.

*First, let him be a man of God. Second, pray together every
day of your life, and third, understand that troubles will try to
tear your love apart, but do not succumb to such evil. God is in
His heaven all the days of your life, and He loves you dearly.*

I love you. Mama

Tears streamed down Sarah Jane's face. Oh, how she missed
Mama and Papa. Sometimes she thought the ache would
never go away. *Select your husband wisely.*

*Mama, I didn't choose Painted Hands. Circumstances chose us.
I pray I never disappoint you, and as long as we are husband and
wife, I will honor him.*

With a deep breath, she replaced the money and thanked
God for His provision. This blessing came at the right time in
light of the upcoming departure of Painted Hands. But her
husband had not left yet, and she would not give up until he
rode away.

"Mrs. Painted Hands."

Sarah Jane heard the familiar male voice but couldn't quite
place the name. "I'll be right with you." She quickly made certain the trunk was in order and climbed down from the
wagon. Of all the people she wished to see, Preacher Sanders
was at the bottom of the list. He'd escaped the typhoid—how
sad. Immediately, she chastised herself.

"Mr. Sanders, how are you?" She feigned cordiality.

"I saw, uh, your husband earlier."

"Yes, you married us, remember?"

He pressed his thin lips together. "Mr. Greenham said
your parents died."

"Yes, sir. I understand many other fine people have perished with the sickness."

"I spoke at more funerals than I care to recall."

"I'm sorry. Mr. Greenham said the epidemic is lessening,"
she said.

"That is my prayer."

Just speak your mind and be gone. "May I ask why you've paid me a visit? Or is this to express your condolences?" Why did peering into the man's face make her irate?

"I've called the committee to a meeting tonight, what's left of them."

"Why do I need to know this?" Exhaustion swept over her. Then she remembered hearing Mr. Greenham state the committeemen might need to meet again if she and Painted Hands returned. If Mr. Sanders simply got on with his business, she'd rest until her husband returned.

"Since your parents were the first to come down with typhoid, I believe you must be carrying it with you."

All thoughts of courtesy vanished. Respect for Mr. Sanders blew with the night breeze. "How dare you make such an accusation? I suggest you leave before I scream for help."

Mr. Sanders took a step back. He looked like the old tom-cat that used to live in Papa's sod barn. He hissed and spit until a person took a step his direction. "Considering the reputation of your husband, I doubt if anyone would listen."

Sarah Jane held her breath while her mind raced with rage. "My husband is a far better man than you could ever be. He knows the meaning of integrity and honor, whereas you hide behind a God whom I doubt you've ever met!"

"You will regret speaking to me in such a manner." His squeaky voice inched higher. "I have my means."

Sarah Jane attempted to calm her nerves. Papa always said anger never solved anything. "Mr. Sanders, you are not welcome here. I'm asking you to leave. If you refuse, I'll ask my husband to file a complaint with the committee."

"No need to ask me." Painted Hands stepped into view. The lantern lit up his reddened features.

"You two are a disgrace," Mr. Sanders said. "As I said earlier, your wagon brought misfortune and death to this wagon train, and I intend to put an end to it."

"Go ahead," Painted Hands said. "While you're at it, you

can include this." He threw his fist alongside the man's jaw, sending him sprawling in the dirt. "That's for bullying my wife. When you get up, I'll give you another one for what you said about her parents."

Sarah Jane grabbed Painted Hands's arm. "He's not worth the trouble. Let him crawl back to his committee."

Mr. Sanders did indeed crawl backward, then shifted to his feet and took off in a dead run. Some of the other wagons had seen and heard the ruckus, but Sarah Jane didn't care. She still trembled.

"I'm so glad you came," she said, taking her breath in quick spurts.

"I've met his kind before. A hypocrite." A rare look of concern etched his brow. "Are you all right? Did he touch you?"

Her breathing refused to slow down. Her legs felt as if they were weighted down with rocks. "I'm tired. So very tired."

Blackness inched over her mind and body, and she gave into the overwhelming urge to sleep.

nine

Painted Hands caught Sarah Jane before she collapsed onto the ground. This was the first time he'd ever touched her, and she was burning with fever. No, not Sarah Jane. He swept her into his arms, noting how light and frail—and incredibly hot—she was. Once she lay on the straw-filled mattress in the back of the wagon, he tried to waken her. She mumbled about needing sleep, but he could not get her to acknowledge him.

You destroy everything you touch.

He ground his teeth against the backdrop of the accusations swirling about in his head. Not this time. Not if he could do anything to stop it. Sarah Jane would not die because of him.

Painted Hands buried his head in his hands. He should have left sooner. Selfishness over his growing feelings for her had ruled his better judgment.

Brushing back a damp curl from her cheek, his callused fingers felt the smoothness of her skin. How he'd longed to be this close these past weeks, but not at the cost of Sarah Jane's health. How could he cool down the fever? Helpless and disoriented, he bit back bitter tears.

"I'll get some water," he said as if she comprehended every word.

Painted Hands scooted back and out of the wagon. Snatching up a towel, he filled a basin. For the next hour, he continuously wiped her face and listened to her occasional delirium. He answered when he could, assuring her she needed rest and he was there for her. He said the things he should have said from the first day of their marriage. What good would it have done, since the ultimate outcome came in her lying ill with typhoid?

"I'm sorry," he said. "Sarah Jane, I never intended for you

to fall prey to my curse."

"Painted Hands," she whispered and lifted her hand.

He grasped it and brought the slender fingers to his lips. Anxiously, he searched her face for signs of consciousness or more of the fever-ravaged confusion.

"Mama, Papa, don't leave me," she said. "He doesn't want me."

Painted Hands sucked in a breath. Guilt attacked him on every side. He'd refused her desire to be his wife. He'd been cruel and heartless in everything he said and did, neglecting to comfort her when her parents died and insisting she not talk to him. He'd wanted to guard her against his curse, and even then his efforts failed.

He remembered the tea she so diligently prepared and spoon-fed to her ma and pa. Lifting the trunk lid, he saw the small bag of dried ginger leaves. His experience with herbs told him this provided little aid for the fever, but it should help the stomach problem that often accompanied typhoid.

The sound of voices outside the wagon seized his attention. He whirled around, recognizing Sanders's high-pitched screech of excitement.

"Right here—he tried to kill me," Sanders said. "All I was doing was offering my sympathy and prayers in regard to his wife's family. We've heard the tales. He's a murderer, I say, and he's dangerous."

Painted Hands took a deep breath to control the bubbling fury. He took a longing glance at Sarah Jane and left her for the storm brewing outside the wagon.

"Sanders, when are you going to tell them the truth?" Painted Hands asked.

Greenham stood with a half dozen other men, but Painted Hands spurned any thought of using his friendship with the wagon master as leverage. "I walked into the campsite to find you accusing my wife's parents of carrying typhoid. You also claimed to have called a committee meeting to cut us out of the wagon train."

"Is this true?" Greenham asked.

Sanders rubbed his bony jaw. "He punched me before trying to kill me."

"I hit you, and I'd do it again, but I never threatened to kill you. Although I wish someone would do me the favor."

"Where's your wife?" Greenham asked. "If she backs up Painted Hands, then I'm for ending this right now."

Painted Hands realized lying about Sarah Jane made no sense. "She's inside the wagon. After I ran Sanders off, she took sick."

"Sick?" one of the men asked.

Staring straight into the man's eyes, Painted Hands saw the fear. "Yes, fever."

"Typhoid," Greenham stated more than asked.

"I think so." Painted Hands hurled an angry glance at Sanders. "What do you have to say now?"

"Cut 'em out," Sanders said, tossing his words to the men beside him.

Greenham stiffened. "After the Bensons, we didn't cut the other families when they came down sick."

"He's a wild man—can't trust 'im." Sanders's voice rose with each word.

"I'd hit you if you insulted my wife," another man said. "Sanders, you called me away from my family, saying this was an important meeting affecting the whole wagon train. This is nothing more than a personal vendetta." The man stepped in front of Sanders. "I hear you asked John Benson for his daughter to marry up with your son. Benson told you no. You want a vote? Fine. Let's do it now." The man stuck out his hand to Painted Hands. "You've never done me wrong, and my vote is for you to stay. I hope some of us can give help in nursing your wife."

Painted Hands shook the man's hand. He didn't even know his name.

"My name is Andrew. I'm feeling right bad about the way you've been treated."

"I appreciate what you've done here tonight," Painted Hands said, and he meant every word.

"Those of you in favor of Painted Hands and his wife staying with the wagons, raise your hand," Greenham said.

Three men voted for them to stay, which left three others opposed.

"I say this couple deserves a chance, especially since we kept the other sick folks," Greenham said.

Sanders sneered. "You don't have a vote."

"What if I quit right now? Then you don't have a scout or a wagon master."

"You'd desert all these people, leaving them to die in the wilderness because of a no-good crazy man?" Sanders tossed Painted Hands a triumphant sneer.

Painted Hands stepped forward. "I'll pull out in the morning with my wife and the fifty head of cattle." He nodded at the three men who had voted in their favor. "I appreciate what you tried to do here, but it won't ever be said that I was responsible for good folks dying." He turned around and headed back to Sarah Jane. For the first time since he'd agreed to marry, Painted Hands felt as if he'd conducted himself as a good man—not a selfish one.

"You take care of your wife," Greenham said. "I'll get your cattle."

"We'll round them up in the morning," Andrew said. "Would you like some company tonight? I could sit with your wife while you sleep a little."

"Thanks, but I don't think I could rest with her sick."

Andrew rammed his hands into his trouser pockets. "I lost my wife and baby boy to typhoid. Can't sleep anyway—might as well see what I can do for you."

Painted Hands studied the man before him. He looked not much older than Sarah Jane. From the haggard look about him, Andrew was hurting real bad. "Sorry about your family. Don't seem fair, does it?"

Andrew shook his head and stared into the darkness. "I reckon the Lord needed 'em, but I miss 'em. . .every minute of the day."

Painted Hands didn't respond, but he knew he'd remember Andrew for as long as he lived. A stranger had seen Painted Hands as a real man without knowing the person inside.

The rest of the night crept by. Painted Hands kept a vigil for Sarah Jane; the idea of sleep never crossed his mind. He thought back over how she'd tried to please him and done little things for him that he failed to acknowledge. So many times she smiled and appeared to be happy even when he was mean. Shame swept over him until he wept.

"I often wish I'd said and done things differently," Andrew said. "I reckon she knows how I'm grieving for her and our son." His voice cracked. "When your wife gets well, be sure to tell her how much you love her."

"I just hope it's not too late," Painted Hands said.

Andrew touched his shoulder. "I'll be praying for you."

Painted Hands wanted to tell him not to bother, but the man had faced enough bad luck in his life without adding to it.

Come morning, the wagon train pulled out, leaving behind Painted Hands and Sarah Jane along with a cloud of dust and bawling cows. They had plenty of water, grazing for the cattle, and provisions. But he longed for herbs to treat the typhoid. White men called the plant coneflower, and he'd seen it cool down the worst of fevers. That meant leaving her, and he feared she'd grow worse while he searched for the wildflowers. All day and through the night, he tended to her. At times he dozed off only to waken sharply with guilt piercing his heart worse than a jagged knife.

Sarah Jane's dress was soaked. He thought long and hard about removing it—wondering about the propriety of it all. Casting aside his doubts, he carefully slid it from her shoulders in hopes this made her more comfortable. She was thin, and he thought back since they'd married and didn't recall seeing her eat much. He stiffened. She'd been ill and either hadn't said a word or didn't pay attention to the symptoms. Pondering over his wife, he assumed she'd pay more attention to someone else's needs than her own. A few nights ago, she'd gone fishing—for him—and after he'd treated her so shamefully.

Maybe he should have tried to tell her the truth about his curse right from the beginning, but it took over a year for the Reverend Crandle to earn his confidence and open up to the truth. Painted Hands dabbed the cloth over Sarah Jane's face and expelled a labored breath. Right now he'd do anything to break this fever.

Coneflower.

The higher the sun climbed in the sky, the higher Sarah Jane's fever. She ranted about things Painted Hands thought were childhood matters, and he'd seen enough typhoid to understand how close she teetered to death. Once she called out for him, and it startled him. The sound of his name on her lips moved him to make a decision. He'd have to leave her long enough to find the reddish-purple wildflower with its healing powers.

"I won't be long, Sarah Jane," he said, caressing her limp hand. "Hold on and fight the typhoid."

In his rush against death, he slipped the bridle over his mare's neck and rode bareback. Digging his heels into the horse's side, he raced across the plain beyond where the cattle from the wagon train had beaten down the grasses. Not a single coneflower broke into his view.

Lord, please. I'm not asking for me but for Sarah Jane.

A stab of realization nearly staggered him. He'd *prayed.* How long had it been?

I have loved you with an everlasting love.

The whisper reminded him of Reverend Crandle's voice but deeper, like the sound of a waterfall. He rolled the words around in his head, grasping and yet fighting their meaning.

"Then tell me what to do." Painted Hands stared up at a cloudless sky. "Take my life. Sarah Jane is innocent of my sins—the curse You have cast upon me."

Sin and suffering do not come from Me.

"Then tell me how to stop it." Painted Hands's voice echoed around him.

You can't.

Sarah Jane deserved to live, to reach her dream of Oregon. She trusted God, even when her parents died. Desperation wrapped a strangling hold around him. Had he gone mad? He, too, must have typhoid. A feverish mind was the reason for the voice. God didn't talk to sinful folks, just good people like Reverend Crandle, Sarah Jane, Andrew, and other folks including his Kiowa family. They all had impressed him with their decency.

"Please don't take Sarah Jane."

Trust Me.

Painted Hands hesitated. If trusting God was all it took to heal Sarah Jane, then he'd trust with every bit of strength in his body. But he'd called out too many times in the past, and God had been silent.

"I beg of You to spare her. Whatever You ask, I will do."

The sounds of insects chorusing over the heated prairie met his ears. The roar in his spirit ceased. Painted Hands relaxed. His hands loosened their grip on the reins, and he trembled. Sweat streamed down his face, more so from the unexplainable encounter than the afternoon sun. Sensing a need to walk, he slid from the mare's back and led her while he sorted through what had just happened.

Suddenly, the horse reared, and the reins were snatched from his grasp. Painted Hands had always prided himself in the way he handled horses, a skill learned from his Indian brothers. In the next instant, the horse broke free and galloped away in the opposite direction of the wagon.

Painted Hands shook his fist. Again he saw the curse of God. Sarah Jane lay dying at the wagon. He couldn't find the wildflowers that would aid in her healing, and now his horse had deserted him. *How can I trust You when You make a mockery of me?*

With grim determination, he headed toward the wagon. Nearly a mile passed with nothing in view but the prairie. Painted Hands continued to search for the coneflower, though he'd looked before his horse deserted him.

Then to the right of him he saw several reddish-purple flowers. They nodded their petaled heads in the warm breeze. Laughing like a boy, he hurried to them and pulled up all he could carry. The entire plant would be made into a tea.

"Thank You," he said, lifting his head to the heavens. He'd ridden right by them earlier, for hoofprints were embedded in the earth.

A surge of energy likened to fresh hope filled his body as he dashed toward Sarah Jane. And when he caught sight of that canvas-covered prairie schooner, he spotted his horse.

He'd found the coneflowers, and the mare had taken off in the opposite direction. How strangely odd and wonderful at the same time. God must love Sarah Jane. Painted Hands realized another peculiar matter. He loved her, too.

Inside the wagon, Sarah Jane lay still; her pallor frightened him. By habit, Painted Hands washed her face, neck, and arms from the basin of water he'd used earlier.

"I have medicine," he said. "Please hold on to life while I brew some tea."

He snatched up the flint and steel fireworks kit and slipped the striker over his finger. Soon he had water heating over a fire and the coneflower steeping, its healing powers spreading through the water. Grasping a mug and spoon, he stirred the tea and allowed it to cool.

Lord, You answered me today, and I thank You. Please heal her. I beg of You.

Inside the wagon, he lifted Sarah Jane's head and spooned the medicine into her mouth, allowing it to trickle down her throat. This had to break the fever—this and prayer.

ten

Sarah Jane fought to open her eyes. She attempted to gather her wits about her, but time and place eluded her. All she could remember was Painted Hands sending his fist into Preacher Sanders's face. She'd tried to stop her husband, but a part of her—a very wicked part of her—gained a sense of satisfaction from the man running off into the night.

I'm sorry, Lord. Vengeance is wrong, and I know it.

Where was Painted Hands? The cloudy haze engulfing her mind started to lift. She remembered he went out into the night, and she waited supper for him. Yes, now things were clearer. She'd found Mama's letter and the money, put it all back into the trunk, then heard Mr. Sanders calling for her. Suddenly, she remembered the irritating man wanting to cut their wagon again. Why couldn't she remember more?

"Sarah Jane?"

Her eyes fluttered. She desperately wanted to open them. Painted Hands spoke her name. Something must be terribly wrong for his voice rang with tenderness.

"Sarah Jane, are you awake?"

She battled the urge to fall back to sleep, but Painted Hands had called her name in a way she'd dreamed. Slowly, Sarah Jane opened her eyes. The blur faded until she saw his face. He looked tired, and she forced a smile. The gesture stole her strength.

"How are you?" he asked.

She mouthed sleepy, and he touched her cheek.

"Don't try to talk," he said. "Rest and get well. You've been very sick."

Sick? She remembered wanting to sleep but nothing else.

78

"You had typhoid, Sarah Jane, but the danger is gone. You need to get well."

She opened her mouth, but he laid a finger to her lips.

"Hush. Go to sleep, and we'll talk later. I have medicine, and it has helped."

Obediently, she allowed her eyelids to close. She'd survived typhoid? How long had she lain ill while Painted Hands cared for her? One question after another inched across her mind with no answers. Later she'd ask the questions, when she wasn't so sleepy. Painted Hands had acted so kind. . . .

When Sarah Jane awoke the second time, evening shadows hugged the wagon. Again her husband sat beside her bed. Had he never left? How dear of him, as though he really cared.

A smile tugged at his lips. "Hello." He reached for her hand. "I've been watching you sleep."

"How long"—the words seemed to drag from her mouth—"have I been ill?"

"Five days."

His reply sent a note of panic throughout her body. Surely she should have died. God must have a reason for sparing her. Now she understood her weakened condition and lack of memory. How good of Painted Hands to nurse her.

"Thank you," she managed. "I'm. . .sorry."

He gathered up her hands into his, and she treasured the sweet gesture. "Sarah Jane, things are going to be different now. I'm the one who's sorry. You nearly died, just when I was about to run off again."

"I'll get well." Speaking pulled at what little strength she mustered. "I want to be a good wife."

"You are. It's me who has failed. Don't try to talk anymore. I have medicine for you, and I've made broth."

Humiliation crept through Sarah Jane as she realized what had been involved with Painted Hands caring for her. She'd been worse than a baby to tend to—spoon-feeding the medicine, bathing her when the dysentery tore through her body. He had ignored his own needs for her sake. Surely the humble task came under God's plan. She thanked God for her husband and for delivering her from the typhoid. Sarah Jane prayed this would be a new beginning for them.

Two days later, he carried her outside the wagon and laid her in the shade beneath the wide branches of a cottonwood tree overlooking the Platte River. While she gazed over the water and listened to the insects, birds, and an occasional cow, Painted Hands washed clothes and straightened the inside of the wagon. The smell of death lingered there, and he opened the flaps at both ends to allow fresh air to whisk away the reminders of typhoid.

While she slept, he found more coneflowers for the healing tea and hunted a rabbit for their supper. She cherished his doting. This was a side of Painted Hands he'd kept secret. He laughed and whistled, and she thought if they never moved from the prairie, she'd be perfectly fine.

"I think I've found a piece of paradise," she said, as he climbed the small bank carrying a dress, shirt, and undergarments from the river.

"It is peaceful."

"Reminds me of Nebraska."

He stopped and gazed out over the prairie, beyond the grazing cattle to where the plains and the horizon met. "Do you want to go back?"

She considered his question. Friends were in Nebraska and a way of life she knew well. But Papa's dreams lay beyond the mountains, and her life was now with her husband. "Nebraska will always be home, but my future is in Oregon. How long before we can travel?"

"You need to grow stronger first."

"I'll drink the medicine all day long, if it will help."

He eased down beside her, holding the wet bundle against his chest. "I refuse to do anything that causes you to be ill again. Sometimes the fever can last for days or weeks. I've seen folks recover from the typhoid, then get something else 'cause their bodies aren't strong."

She studied his blue eyes, matchless to the heavens. "I want us to get to Oregon before the winter snows. When I get tired, I can sleep in the wagon if you're willing to drive." She shrugged. "Providing the cattle keep up a good pace."

He dropped the washing between his legs to the grass below and leaned back on his hands. "I won't take any chances where you are concerned. The journey to Fort Laramie is right ahead, but the mountain pass is difficult for those who are hearty."

"Can't we make better time than the wagon train? We could start earlier in the mornings, and I could make extra bread and bacon so we wouldn't have to stop at noon but move on till nightfall. And we wouldn't need a whole Sunday to wash clothes and hunt, but a half day."

He chuckled and combed his fingers through her curls. "Are you spending all your time fretting over this trip?"

His touch sent her heart racing. This had to be the real love Mama used to speak about. "I do have another idea."

"And what could it be, Sarah Jane? Shall we grow wings and fly like the eagle?"

"I'm serious." She punctuated her words with a nod. "We could sell the cattle at Fort Laramie, unless you want them."

He directed his gaze to the grazing animals. "It would be a sight easier and faster going over the mountains. Ought to keep a milk cow or two."

She smiled from the inside out. "Then we can go soon?"

He gathered up the washing. "I'll think on it, but you need to rest a few more days."

"Two?"

"Three, then we'll talk again."

She sighed. "I want you to see your brother as soon as you can."

He stood and seemed to study her. "Thank you, but Jacob knows I'm coming. Reverend Crandle sent word to him months ago, and my brother knows the perils of the journey."

"I don't want him worrying about you."

"Don't know many folks who've ever done that."

"You have me." When she saw her words left him uncomfortable, she ventured on. "Are you sad about not joining back up with Mr. Greenham?"

His laughter caused a nearby cow to perk her ears. "Only if I'd be missing Preacher Sanders and his committeemen."

"Oh, I declare he has the devil's wit. I'm not judging Mr. Sanders, really, but I feel sorry for him when he meets the Lord."

"True. He is one miserable man, although I met a man named Andrew who understood the meaning of living a Christian life. He stood up for us when the others were afraid of going against Sanders."

"What happened? Do you mind telling me?"

Painted Hands told her everything that occurred the night she fell to typhoid. "Andrew stayed with me until dawn, then helped cut out the cattle. I hope he reaches Oregon and finds a good future."

She thanked God for putting such a good man in their path. Her husband needed to see committed believers who put others before themselves—good folks who lived their faith. Painted Hands had obviously done that very thing while she suffered through typhoid.

In the past few days, she'd noted something wonderful about Painted Hands: a definite tenderness toward her beginning when she first opened her eyes from the typhoid. His new treatment of her had continued. Before, he had erected a barrier in front of him mortared with a fierce determination to keep others out. Now he no longer hid his emotions or said cruel things to her. She prayed it lasted. Earlier, she nearly told him of her feelings, but she feared he'd leave.

With an inner sigh, Sarah Jane watched her husband carry the washing to the wagon. He turned, and she waved. Becoming friends with Painted Hands held a bit of a risk and a challenge. Perhaps he felt the same.

❧

Painted Hands laid the washing over the brush and flat out on the grass to dry. He stole a look at Sarah Jane. Today the color had started to return to her cheeks. She was still weak, and he noticed she'd napped after spending but a few minutes brushing her hair. Such a small task to waste away her energy. He thought of asking if he could brush it for her. He would gladly waste away the hours serving her needs. He craved every moment with Sarah Jane, like a calf trailing after its mother. To make her life easier in this harsh land became his sole purpose. To gaze into her green eyes became his passion. Without question, Painted Hands loved his wife.

A fierce protective instinct settled on him. He peered in every direction, keeping a guarded watch for any animal or bout of nature that might seek to do her harm. His brothers, the Kiowa, flashed across his mind. Some thought they were lazy, for their days were spent in hunting, deepening their skills as warriors, and guarding their homes. Without those traits, a Kiowa could not protect those he loved. Painted Hands understood his purpose as a man, and the realization made him proud and humble at the same time.

The thought of revealing his heart hammered incessantly. Although she held the title as his wife, he'd done nothing to consummate the marriage or encourage her about the relationship—quite the contrary. The spiteful things he'd said to her in the past aroused more guilt than he cared to admit. Tonight he'd apologize for the things he'd said and done. Confessing his heart was another matter. That would have to wait.

Dare he make plans to break camp and risk her health? Selfishly, he wanted nothing better than to head toward Oregon, but Sarah Jane's health was foremost. He'd speak of it again in three days hence. By then he could tell if she were strong enough to continue on to Fort Laramie. The thought of losing her made him shudder. He'd already lost so many before.

Everything you touch is destroyed.

The nagging, despised voice plagued him again. He longed for true peace, the kind he'd felt when he searched for the coneflower—when God spoke to him. Where did the condemning thoughts come from? Reverend Crandle said God loved him and the accusations came from Satan. If he could only believe those words.

That evening Painted Hands milked the cow and urged Sarah Jane to drink a full mug. He'd made butter earlier in the day, and it tasted good on hot biscuits. She even ate a little roasted rabbit with wild onions. Pleased with her determination to gain her strength, he praised her efforts.

"If we are to leave the prairie, then I must eat," she said. "I think you will have to show me how to cook. Your food is so much better than mine."

"You are simply hungry."

"And you prepared a feast."

He watched the firelight dance off her face and wondered how he'd ever managed without her, certainly a strange notion for a man who swore he needed no one. She yawned. Sleepiness filled her eyes.

"Looks like you need some rest." Painted Hands took her plate and glanced at the bit of milk in the bottom of her mug. "Are you going to finish this?"

She covered her mouth to hide another yawn. "You sound like my mama."

"I've assumed a new role."

She drank the last bit and smiled. The mere sight of her warmed his soul.

"I'm looking forward to the day when you don't have to spend all your time taking care of me," she said.

He reached for her hands. "Until then, I'll be your mama. Let me help you to bed."

She slipped her frail fingers into his palms, and he pulled

her to meet him. She stood close enough that he trembled at her nearness, and when she peered into his face with a look of trust and innocence, the urge to kiss her swept over him.

Sarah Jane lifted his hands to her lips, kissing each one. The gesture startled and embarrassed him.

"Why did you do that?" he asked, a bit gruffer than he intended.

"Because these hands took care of me. You fed me, gave me medicine, bathed me, and countless other things." Her melodious voice rang above the night sounds.

"The scars—"

She shook her head. "I feel awkward with how you nursed me, rather discomfited at times, and this is my way of thanking you."

Painted Hands hesitated. The thought of revealing his pain to this precious woman tugged at him. "They are ugly."

"I have never considered them as such. Were they burned?"

"Yes, a long time ago."

"Would you tell me what happened?"

He touched her cheek. He'd never told the whole story to anyone, not even to Reverend Crandle, but that didn't mean the need wasn't there.

"If it's too painful, I understand," she said. "I simply wondered."

Perhaps now the time had come for him to open up a small portion of his past. If he felt worse or she was repulsed, he'd never venture in that direction again. "Once you are in bed, I'll tell you." When she smiled at him again, he thought his heart would burst from his chest. "Do you need for me to help you?"

"I can manage," Sarah Jane said. "I'm getting stronger, you know, and I shan't take long."

eleven

Sarah Jane nestled beneath the warmth of the quilt and called for Painted Hands. She was so very tired, but hearing him talk about himself meant more to her than sleep. They had come so far, and she refused to lose the closeness growing between them.

When he climbed into the wagon carrying the lantern, she couldn't help but admire the familiarity of him: the broad muscles spreading across his shoulders and his beaded hair. His buckskin clothes and moccasins no longer seemed foreign but welcome. A worried frown creased his forehead.

"Sit by me," she said. "I do want to hear your story. Every little bit I learn about you makes me feel as if we are deepening our friendship."

He sat beside the narrow mattress and drew up his knees. She pulled her hands from beneath the quilt to slip into his.

"This is not easy for me, Sarah Jane. I've lived with what happened the night of the fire for many years."

She glanced at the hand covering hers, then back to his face. "I'm listening. I don't want there ever to be anything you hesitate to tell me. After all, you discovered the very worst of me."

Painted Hands squeezed her hand lightly. "You are wrong to think those things. It was an honor to help you." He took a deep breath, and she prayed for his ability to relate the obviously painful memories. "My parents, three sisters, and an older brother—Jacob—lived in the western Kansas territory. I was the youngest. Pa farmed, and we raised animals, and Ma and my sisters tended a garden. My job was to feed the pigs and chickens." He smiled with a look in his eyes that went beyond the here and now.

"I was six years old when I noticed several baby chicks running about the barnyard. In my mind I thought some wild animal would eat them, so I begged my folks to let me bring them inside. They said no, and I went to bed that night very upset. I couldn't sleep and got up to check on those chicks. Everyone else slept, and I knew better than to wake Ma or Pa. I crept out into the cold dark and made my way to the barn. Well, I found the mother hen and discovered her babies were snug and safe under her warm body. I decided to watch the mother hen awhile to make sure she didn't forget about those chicks, and I fell asleep. I woke sometime later to the sight of flames lapping up the cabin and screams from inside. I ran to the front of the cabin and cried out for my ma and pa. Horrible cries echoed around me. I hurried to the well, but the bucket sat inside the house. I remembered Ma asking me to take it outside earlier. I didn't know what to do, and I wanted to save my family. Every time I tried to get inside the cabin, a wall of hot flames stopped me.

"That's when a band of Kiowa on a hunting trip rode up. They were far from their normal territory. They pulled me from the fire, but my family died inside. My hands were burned, and that is how I received my name. For the next ten years, I lived with the Kiowa."

Tears filled Sarah Jane's eyes. "Why haven't you told anyone this? No one should live with this burden."

He released her hand and clenched his fists. "The bucket. I couldn't save any of them because I'd left it inside." He hesitated. "I've often wondered if I did something to start the fire before I left the cabin—knocked over the lantern or failed to see a stray spark from the cook fire."

"You were six years old." Compassion welled in her. "The fire, the deaths were not your fault."

He set his jaw. "I've never seen it that way." He rubbed his face. "I want to know how Jacob got out." Pain poured from his words.

"Now I understand even more about the urgency to get to Oregon. I'm sorry about your family. I wish I could say the right words to make you feel better, to help you see it wasn't your fault."

"I don't think it's possible."

"God can give you peace, Painted Hands. He wants to lift the burden—"

"I've been told the same thing before. I cried out to God that night, but He turned a deaf ear to me."

"He had a reason, although like you, I find it hard not to be angry."

"To send innocent people to a horrible death?" He lifted his hands. "I remember how my hands hurt, as though someone had taken a knife to them. To think, their whole bodies were tortured like that. A loving, caring God would do this?"

The more he spoke, the louder his voice grew. Sarah Jane shivered. She well recalled the night Painted Hands took after Preacher Sanders. Fury hid beneath his soul, a frightening trait for a man she loved.

"I don't know why this terrible thing happened any more than I understand why Mama and Papa died, but I do know two things. Our families are in a better place where there is no pain or fear, and God has a plan for your life and mine. Because I trust in His wisdom and love, I can only serve Him the best way I can."

He said nothing, but the anger remained on his face like a rock etched with time. She hadn't seen this since before the fever, and she feared the pleasant days had disappeared. Painted Hands stood and left the wagon without a good-bye.

Sarah Jane longed to call after him, but she also recognized his need to work through the problems separating him from God. She couldn't be his savior; she could only live her life as Jesus desired and pray Painted Hands found God's grace and mercy.

The following morning, she awoke with a sense of renewed energy. She dressed and realized the simple task did not waste all of her strength. This morning she'd make coffee and breakfast for Painted Hands.

Stepping outside into a marvelous sunrise, Sarah Jane stopped to admire the dusky pink and gray-blue sky of dawn. It felt good to be alive, even with the hazards ahead and the grief of losing Mama and Papa. Her gaze swept about the area for Painted Hands. Normally, he slept under the wagon, but he was neither there nor at the river. She turned her attention toward the cattle and called for him.

Silence.

His spotted mare was nowhere to be found, either. He'd gone hunting, she told herself and ignored the gnawing voice reminding her of last night. Her husband needed breakfast, and she would prepare it for him. When he returned from wherever he'd ridden, she'd ask him about leaving tomorrow. After all, he said three days and they'd talk about beginning the journey again.

The smell of fresh coffee tugged at her growling stomach as well as the aroma of biscuits and frying bacon; yet Painted Hands was nowhere in sight. A twinge of fear wormed up her spine. All the old conversations and his desire to head alone for Oregon worried her. Finally, she sat in the grass and prayed for Painted Hands. She could not eat without him. He'd return shortly; she felt certain. Sleep tugged at her eyelids until they slid shut.

"Sarah Jane. Wake up. Are you ill?"

She opened her eyes to see Painted Hands kneeling beside her. He smelled of the outdoors, of fresh grass and leather. So happy to see him, she wrapped her arms around his neck and kissed his whiskered cheek. Immediately, his eyes widened, and a look of panic swept over him.

"I was frightened." She groped for words. "I. . .thought you'd gone on without me."

"And left you?" He sounded surprised, and she sighed with a splattering of relief.

"Silly, aren't I?"

"I wouldn't just up and leave you, not without making provisions."

She released her hold on his neck. A sinking feeling settled in her stomach. She thought he'd abandoned the idea of going ahead alone. Fierce determination rose in her, and the words spilled out. "I want to go all the way to Oregon with you, Painted Hands. I'm well and able to drive the wagon. We can make good time as we talked about the other night. I promise not to slow you down."

"I'm not good company."

"You're the company I choose."

He crossed his arms. "You're a difficult woman to understand."

She lifted her chin. "Have you ever met a woman you did understand?"

He paused and moistened his lips. "Reckon not."

"This land is terribly hard, Painted Hands, but I know the dreams of Oregon are only weeks away. Please understand that if you want to set up homesteading here by the Platte River and not move another inch toward the mountains, then I want to be right here with you. If you decide to go back to Independence, I want to be with you. If you are ready to head on beyond Fort Laramie and wade through mud and the first signs of snow in the mountains, I'm ready."

He rubbed his whiskered chin. "You're a stubborn and courageous woman."

She shook her head and touched his arm. "I'm not brave, no, not at all. Too many times I feel Mama's desperation. But what I do know is I want to be with you, and I don't care where."

He stared at her for a moment longer. "We could put a few miles behind us day after tomorrow. We will stop at noon for you to rest, and I'll prepare something for us to eat. I'll be watching you, and at the first signs of your faltering, we'll not go a step farther until you sleep."

"So be it." She leaned over and kissed him once more on the

cheek. "Thank you. I intend to be a helpmate, not a burden."

Painted Hands glanced away, as though ignoring her kiss. "I brought down another rabbit, but I want to hunt deer after breakfast."

⁂

Painted Hands raised his shotgun and took aim at the buck in the distance. Meat wasn't the only motive in bringing down the animal. He wanted the hide to make clothes for Sarah Jane. He saw what she wore, and the rugged terrain of the Rockies called for more practical dress than long skirts that weighed down with snow and mud—and proved a hindrance in climbing. If she'd slip into buckskin breeches once her feet hit the mountains, she'd fare much better. For that matter, so would every female journeying the narrow mountain passes.

He chuckled in remembering past wagon trains where proper ladies left Independence donned in heavy skirts, petticoats, and all their other wearisome layers. As the journey lengthened, one layer after another disappeared or was thread-thin, the closer they got to Oregon. Sadly, he recalled the women who swished their skirts too close to the fire or fainted from heat on the prairie when the daytime temperatures soared to one hundred. Because of their choice of clothing, many took sick when the mountain cold chilled them to the bone.

Why a woman chose to make this trip puzzled him. Separated from friends and family, realizing the death of loved ones, struggling with day-to-day survival, and facing their own female sensibilities was a mystery. Sarah Jane's words inched across his mind. Did the hundreds of women who started out across the wilderness feel like her? Did being with their husbands mean more to them than danger? He was uncomfortable with Sarah Jane's feeling so strongly about him, but her commitment left him proud. Could he claim the same about her?

She'd be clothed properly, for sure, and he'd treat her as he wanted to be treated. Looks said more than words, and he'd seen something in her eyes, a light that seemed to say she cared for him. He had no idea why, unless his nursing her had brought about sentiments of gratitude. But if he thought back to before the typhoid, she tried to please him then, too.

Sarah Jane scared him worse than walking up on a she-bear with cubs.

After taking down the buck, Painted Hands positioned the animal atop his horse and led the mare back to the wagon. Again, as he had so many times in the past, he pondered the situation with his wife—his wife in name only. If he could fault her, he'd feel much better. If she had reacted to his story with anything but kindness, he could have justified leaving her at Fort Laramie. Sarah Jane wasn't perfect, but she stood on the border, causing him to wonder if she was an angel sent to make his miserable existence a little easier to bear. If he affixed his mind to that way of thinking, he'd have to acknowledge God.

twelve

Sarah Jane had busied herself all morning, and now she read from Papa's Bible. Her perch beneath the cottonwood facing the river had become her favorite spot during her recuperation. She could become very lazy here, mesmerized by the gentle flow of the water and the placid scene of grazing cattle. She opened the Bible to one of Mama's favorite passages—the book of Ruth. The ancient Moabite woman's journey to a new home and her devotion to God filled Sarah Jane with renewed hope for her marriage.

Papa always said things happened for God's reason and not our own. At the time, Sarah Jane believed him, though since her marriage, she'd contemplated the wisdom of Papa's statement. One moment she was filled with despair and certain Painted Hands planned to leave her at Fort Laramie; in the next he acted as if he cared. She wanted to look expectantly to the future, but she wished God would give her a glimpse of it. Trust was a heavy dose of medicine to one who lacked patience.

Closing the Bible, she stood and headed back to the wagon. There Painted Hands bent over a deer. He'd skinned the hide and set it aside, then deftly sliced up the meat. She could cure it with the extra salt, but her curiosity came with what he intended to do with the hide.

"I'm going to tan it," he said. "You need some good buckskin for the mountains." He filled a second bucket with the venison. "We're going to stay an extra two days here to get it started."

Buckskin? Mama and Papa will roll over in their graves. "I have clothes, Painted Hands."

"I know, but they aren't suitable for the mountains." A

smile greeted her. "Once you get used to them, you might never wear a dress again."

"So will I wear a buckskin dress like an Indian woman?"

He laughed long and loud. "No, Sarah Jane. These will be breeches and a shirt. They won't wear out, and the going will be easier."

I have to be excited about this. "No one will be able to tell us apart."

"Oh, I imagine there will be a few differences."

Sarah Jane flushed hot, and it had nothing to do with the heat of the day or a fever.

Sarah Jane wanted to leave the peaceful site by the Platte River, but she realized the need for a few extra days of rest, and the thought of watching her husband prepare a hide for clothing purposes sounded interesting. In fact, she decided to record each step in Mama's journal.

Painted Hands began the process once the meat had been sliced and salted. He prepared a mixture of the deer's brains and liver with a little fat in a kettle over a low fire.

"Are you going to eat that?" she asked.

"Did you want to?"

"Not exactly, although I guess if I was hungry enough, I'd eat anything."

He stirred the mixture before answering. "Once it's cooked for about an hour, it will be ready to use in the tanning."

She had so many questions, but she knew how he felt about them. "Will I bother you by wanting to learn how this is done?"

He stopped stirring. "I'll make you a deal. You watch me do this, and if there is something you don't understand, go ahead and ask."

She shrugged. "All right."

"The wisdom comes in knowing when to observe and when to pose your questions."

Her eyes widened.

Maybe the idea of recording the instructions could wait until another time, but she would at least begin now.

"It's very simple," he continued. "If you ask a good question, I'll answer. If you ask a bad one, then you have to eat the brains and liver mixture." Not a muscle moved on his face.

Sarah Jane hid her mirth. "Agreed, and I'll provide a spoon for you, too."

They laughed together, and it felt good. Really good.

In the late afternoon, Painted Hands staked the hide onto the ground, stretching it taut as he worked. He divided the brain and liver mixture in half, rubbing it into one side, then the other with an old rag. With his hands and a smooth, rounded rock, he worked the mixture thoroughly over every part of the hide. He scooted back on his knees and appeared to study every inch of it. Then he released the stakes from the hide and folded it up.

"That's all I can do for today." He peered over her shoulder as she wrote. "Tomorrow I'll wash the hide and stake it again."

"Stretch it, too?" she asked, then immediately wondered if she should have waited.

"Yes, it will shrink if I don't." He grinned. "Are you going to write a book about the Oregon adventure?"

"I'm pondering the matter. Our children and grandchildren might find it interesting." The mention of children invited warmth to rise from her neck to her cheeks.

He said nothing, but the silence felt like a wall of rock between them.

"I'll fix our supper," she said. "The deer will be a welcome change."

"While you're tending to that, I need to make a travois, a wide one."

She lifted a questioning gaze.

"The hide will need to dry in the sun. No faster than the wagon moves, I plan to stretch it out over a travois."

"Did you learn that from the Kiowa?"

"No." He chuckled. "I don't know if it's been done this way before. Tanning hides is done in a camp—and by the women."

"Then I'd better pay attention."

Once the meat started to sizzle in the pan, Sarah Jane milked the cow. She'd assumed most of her chores by now, but she appreciated that Painted Hands was concerned about her health. When they started on the trail again, she planned to share every bit of the work with him.

"The color is back in your face," he said, reaching for another biscuit.

Grateful for his notice, she responded with a smile.

"Sarah Jane," he began a few minutes later. "There's a matter between us we should talk about."

This was not his usual manner. She swallowed hard with the knowledge that he must have a serious topic of discussion. *Do not think the worst.*

"We're married, but we're not living like married folks."

She nodded and sensed her cheeks were aflame.

"I'm a man, and I could easily claim my rights as a husband, but I won't until I can see myself as a fitting person for you."

She blinked back a tear. He'd already proved to her that he was good and kind. What more did he dare accomplish? "To me you are more than I ever thought possible in a man or a husband."

"How many men have you known? Your pa and his acquaintances?"

"That's a fair amount." She twisted a loose thread on her apron hem. "Doesn't matter to me how many or whom. God knows best. You're a fine man, Painted Hands, and I'm proud to be your wife."

He set his plate on the ground and stood. With a heavy sigh, he turned and stalked away into the darkness.

Must he always run when things don't suit him? She wanted to shout at him to come back—to talk about the matter of their marriage—except the words refused to spill from her lips. Without asking, Sarah Jane realized he'd not make a move back to the wagon until she'd gone to bed. In the past, moments like these made her stomach churn, but not tonight. God had given her a peace about Painted Hands.

Mend his broken heart, O God. He blames himself for his family's deaths and most likely too many other things.

The following morning, Painted Hands acted as though nothing had happened. He appeared friendly enough, but he'd put a definite distance between them.

After breakfast, he disappeared again without a word. Sarah Jane elected to bathe and wash her hair. An amazing calm cradled her, and she found herself singing.

At noontime, Painted Hands returned and announced he planned to work on the hide. She sat on the opposite side of him, relishing in the closeness while watching him work with his hands. Soon he had the hide washed to his perfection and staked in the sun to dry. Once more, he left on his horse.

Where does he go? What does he do?

ঌ

Painted Hands slipped his Bible from his saddlebag and found a soft place to sit and read. He hadn't told Sarah Jane where he'd been spending his time, and if he allowed himself to be honest, he'd confess his natural rebellious instinct was the reason. The ill-tempered side of him claimed he deserved his privacy. The tender side of him understood she'd worry, and he should spare her any discomfort.

Since her illness, he'd wanted to find reasons for his existence, the answers as to why his life had gone from one bad turn to another. All of Reverend Crandle's words flowed through him, which was why he'd sneaked away to read those passages important to his old friend. Always he came back to Psalm One. The words of David were like a guidebook to Painted Hands, and though he fought the power of God in his life, he couldn't discount the wisdom.

Blessed is the man that walketh not in the counsel of the ungodly, nor standeth in the way of sinners, nor sitteth in the seat of the scornful. But his delight is in the law of the Lord; and in His law doth he meditate day and night. And he shall be like a tree planted by the rivers of water, that bringeth forth his fruit in his season; his leaf also shall not wither; and whatsoever he doeth shall prosper. The ungodly are not so; but are like the chaff which the wind driveth away. Therefore the ungodly shall not stand in the judgment, nor sinners in the congregation of the righteous. For the Lord knoweth the way of the righteous; but the way of the ungodly shall perish.

Painted Hands looked out over the prairie—quiet, peaceful, as he wanted to feel inside. God had answered his prayers on this very terrain and showed him the coneflowers. In turn, the tea made from the wildflowers helped save Sarah Jane's life. But the other tragedies of the past filled him with bitterness.

He couldn't deny God, but he couldn't give himself over to trust, either—not as he once did. If the answers to his miserable life would miraculously appear, he could understand why. Was he cursed by the same God who said He loved all His creation?

. . .the way of the ungodly shall perish.

God said the way of sinners would perish, but sinners could receive forgiveness. Painted Hands remembered enough from his own Bible study and his years with the Reverend Crandle that acknowledgment of wrongdoings initiated confession. Then repentance had to occur before forgiveness could take place. What had he done so wrong that God chose to strike him down and the ones he loved? Always the same questions. Always the same silence.

And if he declared love for his wife, God would take her, too. That fear alone halted a move in Sarah Jane's direction. He ached to hold her, touch her smooth, soft cheeks the way he did when she lay burning up with fever. His mind sped with the words he wanted to say but couldn't. He recalled the treasured times he'd let himself enjoy her company. Those moments were sealed for the bleak future.

She wanted to record the events along the trail to Oregon for their children and grandchildren. Painted Hands desired the same and more. A longing so deep and passionate assaulted him whenever he thought of a green-eyed child calling him Papa.

৯

After dusk, Painted Hands returned to the wagon site. He seated himself by the cook fire. His shoulders sagged; when the firelight illuminated his face, lines deepened around his eyes.

Compassion moved Sarah Jane, but she was weary from wrestling with her own emotions.

"Tomorrow is your last day before we leave this place." His gaze stayed fixed on the reddened embers.

"I'm ready." She hoped her words sounded optimistic.

"Nothing you want me to tend to?"

She shook her head. An urgency in her spirit moved her to say more. "I'm sorry I've said things that make you want to stay away."

He stared into the fire, his features like stone. "You, Sarah Jane, have always done what is good and right. I'm the restless, wild one."

"You're wrong." She spoke clearly in the night. "I pray you one day discover how blessed I am." As she expected, Painted Hands did not respond. "Think of what you've done for me. You volunteered to help strangers with deadly typhoid. You married me when Preacher Sanders demanded it. You helped me nurse Mama and Papa and spared me the pain of preparing them for burial. You took care of me when you could have left me behind. Every minute of the day, you ignore your needs for mine. If that is your description of restless and wild, then I hope someday to claim such honorable traits."

He rubbed his palms. "I am cursed, Sarah Jane. Whatever I touch is destroyed. I can't allow another human being to suffer because of me."

Folks were not cursed. What did he mean? How could she make him understand that life held many tragedies? Good and bad fell on everyone.

"I'm going to check on the cattle," he said. "Go on to bed when you're tired."

She stood and laid her hand on his arm. "You can do all you will to stop me from caring, but I'm determined. Run as far from me as you can, but I won't stop praying."

"You're a fool!"

His words pierced her heart. "Perhaps you're right. Some days I want to give up and resign myself to watching you leave me. But when I consider what I'd lose, I pray for more strength." Standing, she climbed into the wagon and willed herself to sleep.

On the morning of their last day along the Platte River, Painted Hands took a rough stone and rubbed it into the entire hide. Sarah Jane silently recorded his every move. In the late afternoon, he made a loop of rope and worked the hide back and forth through it. Once he finished, he heated water and lowered the hide into it.

"I'll take care of this before we leave."

"What's next? Can I help you?" She realized he abhorred unnecessary quizzing, but frustration in dealing with him worked at crushing her spirit.

"To do this properly, I have to make sure it's stretched out tight." He paused. "I hope my idea of using a travois is not a mistake."

She thought a minute. "Could you fix the hide to the top of the wagon?"

"Possibly." He was using his cold, unfeeling tone. She'd gotten rather used to it, but that didn't mean she liked it or embraced the silence.

Late that night, Sarah Jane woke to the sound of crashing thunder. The intensity shook the wagon. She glanced out at the night sky and gasped at the vivid display of jagged lightning across the dark heavens. In less than a second, thunder pounded again. High winds seized the canvas and whipped it to the outside. She heard Painted Hands stirring about the travois and hurried to join him.

"A bad storm is upon us," he said, releasing the deer hide and hoisting it into his arms. "Make sure everything is brought inside."

She hustled about to store their belongings from the impending storm. She remembered when they'd been scarcely out of Elm Grove and a prairie storm besieged the wagon train and sent the cattle stampeding. She and Mama had huddled inside like frightened chickens until it was over. Lightning had struck one of the wagons nearby and quickly set fire to the canvas top. This storm looked no less intimidating.

The wind wove its way across the land. The whole earth rumbled with no reprieve in sight. Sarah Jane and Painted Hands climbed into the wagon with the lighted lantern and sat on the mattress. The wind whistled, and the wagon rocked. Then the rains came as though the storm clouds desired to drown earth's inhabitants. This must be how the people felt outside Noah's ark.

"Sounds like we're under a waterfall." She refused to think about a swirl of floodwaters sweeping them away into the Platte River. "Are we on high enough ground?"

"I believe so," Painted Hands replied. He sounded neither hopeful nor downcast.

The cattle milled about, crying out with the upheaval in nature. As a little girl, she'd covered her ears during storms, but none of those frightful memories compared with the roar outside the wagon. Sarah Jane wrapped her arms about her and shivered.

"I hope the cattle don't stampede," she said. "Are there any buffalo nearby?"

"There's nothing we can do if the cattle get spooked or a herd of buffalo runs us over."

"Well, I'm scared!"

"I figured as much." He picked up the quilt from the bed and draped it around her shoulders. "Keep warm, Sarah Jane, or you will have fever again."

Above the deafening roar of the storm, another drumming against the earth assaulted her ears. The cattle. They were running. She held her breath. Any moment she expected the wagon to topple over while she and Painted Hands faced the hooves of frightened cows.

The thunder and lightning finally ceased, but the downpour continued until dawn. This was supposed to be the day they'd pack up camp and move toward the Northwest, but instead, it would be spent in rounding up cattle on a water-soaked prairie. Luckily the oxen were close by.

"I can ride Papa's horse and help you," she said.

"You stay here. The extra day of rest is a good thing." With those words, he tramped across the mud and rode out.

Somewhat agitated with his refusal, she easily fell back to sleep and dreamed of Oregon and its claim to being near heaven. Midmorning, she woke to the soft sounds of more rain. The longer it fell, the more it picked up momentum. The river had risen considerably last night. Would it reach the banks and sweep her away? Shaking her head, she vowed to push away the worrisome thoughts.

Painted Hands was a strong man, but the constant exposure to the elements gave her cause for alarm. As long as it continued to rain, she couldn't make him coffee. *Keep him safe, Father, and help him find the cattle.*

Late afternoon, the rain let up. Sarah Jane affixed her skirts to well above her ankles and stepped out beneath a cloudy sky. Her gaze flew to the river, where the water nearly crested.

A hint of light attempted to peek through the dismal gray, but what she needed was a rainbow. She picked through the buffalo chips they had stacked inside the wagon last night to build a fire. Cooking for Painted Hands kept her mind and body occupied until he returned.

Just before dusk, she saw him ride from the east. He drove a number of cows; perhaps all had not run into parts unknown.

"We lost five of your pa's cattle," he said, swinging down from his mare. Water dripped from his hat, beard, and clothes.

"They are our cattle," she said. "And I was more worried about you than the animals."

Painted Hands lifted a brow.

"Please don't doubt me. You're a sight more important than"—she waved her arm toward them—"those cattle."

"Are you always looking after other folks?" The strained muscles in his face challenged her.

Sarah Jane stiffened. "Yes, most times, even those who don't care one way or the other." She bent and poured him a mug of coffee. "This hasn't been made too long. It might thaw out your heart." She thrust the mug at him, and he chuckled.

"Guess I had that one coming."

"Good, because I'm in no mood to apologize."

Early the following morning, the day of their departure, Sarah Jane woke with anticipation to be gone again. She dressed and collected her journal for already she smelled coffee and biscuits.

Painted Hands had mounted the hide, hair side down, onto the wide travois with strips of leather. About every six inches, he fastened a piece of it to the travois. To Sarah Jane, the deer hide could not possibly shrink. With a knife, he began to scrape the pieces of flesh and fat still attached. Twice the hide nearly dried, but he added warm water to his work. Once he had finished, he stood back.

"It needs to dry for about two days. Then I'll soak it again and scrape the hair side."

"I see it takes awhile, like most things we value."

He set his jaw and cleaned his knife on the grass.

Sarah Jane decided tanning the deerskin was much like God laboring over troubles that plagued Painted Hands. Every step He scraped off the ugliness from the past and worked on making a new man who would eventually step forward with purpose and direction. Maybe then he'd want to be a real husband.

thirteen

The first day on the trail came easier than Sarah Jane anticipated. A tinge of bittersweetness enveloped her when she thought of leaving the peaceful spot on the prairie with its lush grasses and wildflowers. She could have easily lived out her years there—building a home by the Platte River and raising babies. Of course, harsh winters, summer twisters, and flash floods would soon give cause for regret. So would life almost anywhere she lived.

She shook her head. Longing for a life that might never be hers was foolish. First in order was her husband's spiritual life; all the other problems lagged sadly behind.

The oxen plodded ahead, and the sun grew hotter in the sky. She'd cast aside her petticoat for only her dress in the heat, not caring a bit if she came upon a gathering of women. My, how her priorities had changed. She grinned at the thought of wearing buckskin. Next she'd be in moccasins and living in a tepee. Preacher Sanders would hold a revival if he learned about her new way of life.

Over to her right, Painted Hands drove the cattle with an occasional holler. The scent of the animals had made Mama ill, but Sarah Jane didn't mind. After the stench of death, she could handle about anything. The tall grass made them fat, which should help bring a fair price at Fort Laramie. Then Painted Hands would be free to roam about as he pleased.

"Isn't it wonderful to be moving again?" she called to him.

He nodded and waved. At least he acknowledged her. The oxen trudged on ahead while the road bent and wound with the river. The solitary wagon ambled on, passing Chimney Rock with its single peak like an outstretched arm reaching to the sky and on to Scotts Bluff. Painted Hands figured it would take them about a week to reach Fort Laramie; he was certain Mr. Greenham had pulled out to the mountains by now. Not that she cared; she'd rather not see any of them again.

At noon, Painted Hands stopped the cattle to keep his word for her to rest while he prepared a meal. Today they planned to eat leftover biscuits and bacon from breakfast and drink water to wash it all down.

"I'm going to scout around while you nap," he said. "Do you know how to use your pa's shotgun?"

"Yes, Papa taught Mama and me before we left Nebraska."

"Good. I meant to ask you before. Don't be afraid to use it."

Why had he waited so long to find out? It wasn't as though he hadn't left her alone in the past. "Is there trouble ahead?"

He finished his food and set the tin plate on the ground. "Fort Laramie can be rough with white men and Indians."

Had he decided to leave her there? "I can take care of myself." Irritation crept into her thoughts. Painted Hands had more unexplainable moods than a woman.

He chuckled, and it fueled her frustration. "What's so funny?"

"Your stubborn attitude."

"Me?" Sarah Jane squeezed the reins. "Sounds to me like you're ready to leave me at Fort Laramie, but first you have to make sure no one is going to pull a gun on me."

He swung a glare at her. "I haven't decided."

"I'm so glad you're in charge of my future. Let me tell you this, and don't you lose sight of it. I'm going to Oregon, and if you won't take me, then I'll find my way with another wagon train."

"I have no doubt you would take out over those mountains alone."

"Must you always be so smug?" Sarah Jane bit back another ugly remark, one that involved not needing any man to protect her.

"I know a few more things about this country than you."

"Wonderful, but your knowledge doesn't make you an expert on what's best for me."

Painted Hands snatched up his shotgun and stood. He towered over her. "A husband is in charge of his household."

She struggled to her feet. Rage pushed through her veins. "You have to be a husband first."

Painted Hands whirled around and stomped off toward his spotted mare.

"You always run," she said. "For once, I'd like for us to talk through something."

He kept right on without hesitation. He slid onto his horse bareback and raced out across the flat terrain, leaving a cloud of mud spitting behind him. Let him ride until he fell off the edge of the earth. Making her own way to Fort Laramie and on to Oregon wasn't impossible, and she could take care of herself without him or anyone else.

Suddenly, remorse seized her for the impetuous words she'd flung at Painted Hands. After all he'd done for her, and she repaid him with sarcasm. She'd committed to reflect Jesus in her life, but her pride had stepped in and taken over. Sarah Jane focused her attention on the direction where he'd ridden. A part of her wanted to saddle Papa's horse and go out after him. The longer she waited, the more impatience needled her. Guilt laced every thought. Watching the prairie didn't bring him any closer, either.

❧

Sarah Jane's fury tore at Painted Hands. *You always run.* He didn't know his wife was capable of such anger, and oddly enough, seeing her red-faced offered relief. His original opinion of her was that she'd allow him to domineer her every move. Today she'd proven otherwise.

You always run.

She was right. He'd spent most of his life running from some kind of truth. When life gave him sorrow, he took off in the opposite direction. He'd started as a child with the Kiowa when their different ways frustrated him or when memories plagued his tormented mind, and he persisted in the habit with the Crandles and now Sarah Jane. They should have named him Runner.

The Reverend Crandle had told him a man faces his problems head-on and asks God to help him with the solution. Painted Hands understood the wisdom in those words, because the running labeled him less of a man. At one time, Reverend Crandle asked him to dwell on the good times in the past and give the bitterness to God. The idea of facing the problems and remembering the good sounded easy in one breath and insurmountable in the next. So he'd done nothing but continue in the same pattern. Now feelings for Sarah Jane and the hope she built in him of being a whole man moved him to step out in faith—yes, faith in the God who refused to let him go. If Painted Hands pondered the matter, would his days be any more miserable with Him than his current meaningless existence?

Once again giving his life to Jesus Christ, with the understanding there would be no turning back, frightened him. There—he'd admitted it. Fear of the unknown kept him bound tighter than a heavy rope.

You are not alone.

Painted Hands recognized the voice, and it wasn't the one Reverend Crandle called the accuser.

Lord, forgive me for not having the strength to stay close to You. I'm a broken man, weak and lower than a snake, and I can't do this alone. So many questions pound my head and heart that I'd rather run forever than face them squarely. Help me, Lord. I beg of You.

A verse sprang from his mind, one he remembered reading many times in the past. This time the words held clarity, and he reached out to hold onto them with all his might.

"Come unto Me, all ye that labour and are heavy laden, and I will give you rest."

"Thank You," he whispered.

Painted Hands stopped his horse and eased the mare back from whence he came. With a renewed commitment to God, he must mend his relationship with Sarah Jane—his wife.

❧

Sarah Jane shielded her eyes. There, off to the southwest, someone approached. She studied the figure heading her way until she realized there were several riders. Her heart pounded hard against her chest.

Indians! She counted seven of them—seven fierce-looking men. *Papa's shotgun.* She had to dig it out from underneath some boxes. Why hadn't she done that sooner? By the time she found it, they'd be here. Her legs threatened to give way. Her mouth grew dry. Trembling, she grabbed the side of the wagon for support. Her gaze swept around the campsite. A knife lay just inside the wagon. She forced herself to release her grip and snatch up the weapon.

Dear Lord, is this the end?

The Indians wore breechcloths. One wore a sleeveless shirt, similar to the buckskin Painted Hands wore but with more beadwork and fringe. She'd seen the Sioux when still traveling with Mama and Papa, and these Indians looked different. One of the men wore a black animal skin hat. Their bronzed bodies glistened in the sun, their muscles rippling like the flow of the Platte River. She recalled the horrific tales of warring Indians and shuddered.

While she leaned against the side of the wagon, they formed a half circle around her. The one who wore the hat laughed and slid from his horse. Sarah Jane raised the knife, although her hand shook so badly, she almost dropped it.

"What do you want?" she asked in a voice that quivered like a leaf in the wind.

In a language foreign to her, the Indians exchanged words and grunts. They pointed at her, Papa's horse, and the cattle. Even if Painted Hands returned, what could he do? Maybe they were Kiowa. Why hadn't she asked Painted Hands to teach her the language? The one wearing the hat stepped closer. She lifted the knife higher. A sick feeling swept over her.

"Take the cattle." The sound of her voice wrapped fear around her heart. "I'll stab this knife into your heart if you come any closer."

The hat-wearing Indian yanked the weapon from her hand and grabbed her arm.

Sarah Jane screamed. She beat her fists against his chest, and when he lowered his grasp to her waist, she continued to pound any part of his body she could reach with her fists. Laughter rose from him and the other Indians. He pulled her toward his horse. He smelled of filth and animals. She kicked, then bit him before a dirty hand clamped over her mouth.

Dear God, help me!

The Indian carried her toward his horse, while the others rummaged through the wagon.

A shot fired.

She held her breath, praying.

The voice of Painted Hands rang out over the sultry air, but not in English. The Indians must be Kiowa, but Painted Hands had said the prairie was not their home. She cringed. There were too many of them to fight. He'd be hurt. *Help us, dear God.*

❧

Painted Hands had seen the tracks before he raced back to the wagon. The Indians were Cheyenne, and Sarah Jane was alone. They'd pick the place clean, drive away the cattle, and ride off with his wife—if they did not choose to kill her. Panic twisted through him, then anger. This was his fault. He'd left her alone to face any danger, as he'd done so many times in the past. He had to get to her, fast.

"Please, God, no." His heels dug into the horse's side, urging the mare faster. He fired his shotgun into the air at the sound of her screams. The image of Sarah Jane abused by the Indians attacked his senses. "Sarah Jane!"

"Neaahtove!" *Listen to me.* Painted Hands spoke the words

in Cheyenne. "Éneoestse!" *Stop.*

The warrior holding on to Sarah Jane laughed. "Emoonahe." *She is pretty.*

Painted Hands fought his anger. "She is my wife." They would not take her; he'd die trying.

"Why do you speak our language?" The warrior's eyes narrowed.

"I lived with the Kiowa for ten years. I learned your language through a Cheyenne brother."

The warrior held a firm grip on Sarah Jane. Fear etched her delicate features.

"Netonesevehe?" *What is your name?*

"Painted Hands." Perspiration trickled down his face.

The warrior glanced at the scarred hands of Painted Hands, then back to his face. "I want to buy this woman."

"She is not for barter." He took a step toward Sarah Jane and touched her stomach. "Naneso." *My child.* Painted Hands realized the warrior would not let Sarah Jane go easily. "You can have five of the cattle."

The warrior sneered. "The cattle are already mine."

"We are brothers."

The man stiffened. "For long time, Kiowa and Cheyenne at war."

"The Kiowa and Cheyenne made peace eight years ago."

The other warriors began to talk until the man silenced them. "You know our ways. Five of the cattle are not enough."

"Ten."

"And the horse."

Neither the horse nor the cattle were his to give away, but he had no choice. "Agreed."

"Twenty cattle."

"I said ten."

"Ten and the horse, and we leave the woman," the warrior said.

Painted Hands studied the Indian before him. If he hadn't

bargained in Cheyenne, he'd have been killed, and they'd have Sarah Jane. He nodded at the warrior and headed back to retrieve John Benson's horse. When Painted Hands returned, he held out the bridled horse and eyed the warrior squarely.

"My wife," Painted Hands said. The warrior released her, and Painted Hands pulled her to him. "We are brothers. Let me have my woman cook for you."

The Indian nodded and motioned for the others to cut out the cattle.

"Are you hurt?" Painted Hands asked Sarah Jane.

"No." Sarah Jane trembled so that her skirt shook.

He drew her closer, and she laid her head on his chest. If not for watching the Indians taking the cattle, he'd have kissed her.

"They are taking ten head of cattle and your pa's horse," he said.

She nodded and pressed her lips together. "They can have all the cattle."

"I was ready to give them everything we have. And a belly full of lead, if that's what it took."

"They're leaving?" she asked.

"They need food. Are you able to cook for them?"

"We have the salted deer. I'll cook plenty—anything to make sure they don't come back."

Sarah Jane sliced off hunks of the venison and fried them and baked biscuits. After the Cheyenne ate their fill, Painted Hands watched as the Indians made their way to their horses. The Indians shouted and took out across the plain with the cattle. Two of them held the chickens. In the next instant, they were a speck of dust disappearing over the prairie. He pulled his wife next to him.

"Thank you, Painted Hands," she said. "I'm sorry for what I said to you."

He rested his chin on her head. "I'm not. It was the truth. Tonight, after we've settled down from supper, I want to talk."

"Of course." Her eyes glistened with tears. "The Indians, are they Kiowa?"

"No, Cheyenne. I learned their language some years before."

"Praise God," she whispered. "I've never been so frightened."

"He wanted you for himself." Painted Hands expelled a heavy breath. What if he'd failed?

Her face paled. "I would have rather died. Why—why did you touch my stomach?"

"Sarah Jane. Forgive me, but I told him you carried my child."

She wrapped her arm around his waist. "There is nothing to forgive. Once again you have saved my life." Her soft weeping tugged at his heart.

"You forget my anger is what put you in danger. I'll never leave you like that again. If I need to hunt, you will go with me."

She snuggled against his chest. If he died tonight, he'd keep this moment forever sealed in his mind.

"Let's leave this place," he said. "I wouldn't want those Indians to forget I called them brothers."

In a short time the wagon meandered in the opposite direction from where the Cheyenne drove the cattle. He couldn't keep his gaze off Sarah Jane, and whenever he stole a glimpse of her, she was looking at him. The desire to tell her of his love and his renewed faith nearly burst from his chest.

The afternoon hours sped by as Painted Hands relived the scene with the Cheyenne. Repeatedly, he praised God for rescuing his precious wife. Every time he considered what might have happened to her, a fierce, protective resolve shattered his past treatment of her.

"Do you want me to tie my horse to the wagon?" he asked. "I'd like to sit next to you."

She pulled back on the reins and called to the oxen. "Does that answer your question?"

fourteen

Sarah Jane prepared a dried-peach cobbler that night, adding a pinch of cinnamon and a hunk of the precious butter. Mama had always said the best way to keep a man happy was to feed him well.

"You're a good cook, Sarah Jane," he said, scooping up more of the peach cobbler.

"Thank you. I had a good teacher with Mama."

"You miss her badly, don't you?"

She blinked back the wetness. "Doesn't seem like they're really gone. I hope I don't ever forget the good times—and the love we shared."

"I understand. My family lives in my dreams."

"Oh, but soon you will be reunited with your brother."

He smiled. "Sometimes I wonder if Jacob will look at all as I remember."

"I'm excited for you." She poured him another mug of coffee. "Your meeting will be grand."

"He's not married, at least not yet. So he will have a brother and a sister."

His words touched her, and warmth flooded her face. She didn't know how to respond without becoming emotional. *He must have changed his mind about leaving me at Fort Laramie.*

"Sarah Jane," he began. "While I was gone today, I made a decision."

She met his gaze and studied him through the amber firelight.

"I haven't been good to you, and saying I'm sorry doesn't cover all the ways I've wronged you. But I am sorry. I told you about the fire. You should know other things about me, and

I'll tell you of them someday. You already know I'm not a talkative man." He released a sigh and stared into the fire. "While living with Reverend Crandle, I made a decision to follow Christ, but I turned my back on Him. See, folks accused me of murdering a family, and the Reverend Crandle took up for me. Because of his commitment to me, he lost his church. It didn't seem right for God to allow it. I was bitter, angry, so I signed up as a scout for Greenham's wagon train. During that time, the reverend tracked down Jacob and found out he'd gone to Oregon."

"Have you seen the reverend since?"

Painted Hands nodded. "Just before the wagon train left Independence. He had a new church in Independence."

"How wonderful for him and his wife."

He paused for a moment. Should she have said nothing while he spoke, or should she prod him?

"What was your decision?" Sarah Jane pulled her shawl tighter around her shoulders.

"I figured since God hadn't given up on me, I needed to follow Him. He answered my prayers to help me find the coneflower when you were sick with typhoid, and He saw fit to save you."

"Oh, Painted Hands, I'm so glad."

"I'm a stubborn man, prone to keeping my troubles to myself, but with God's help, I'm going to change." He looked up at her through saddened eyes. "I want to be a good husband, Sarah Jane, if you'll have me and have patience. I nearly got you kidnapped or killed by those Cheyenne, and I'm powerful ashamed."

Her chest felt heavy, but she was determined not to cry. "I think we both learned a lot today." She hesitated. How did he feel about her beyond honoring his wedding vows? Love was a gift, a vow on her part, not his. "I love you, Painted Hands. I have for some time, but I was afraid to tell you."

His face tightened, and he inhaled deeply. He reached out

for her. "And I love you." He held her close, and when she peered up at him, he lowered his head and brushed his lips against hers.

Sarah Jane had never been kissed by any man other than Papa, who had sometimes graced one on the top of her head. Warm and sweet best described the tender embrace of Painted Hands. If she lived to see her great grandchildren, she'd never forget his endearing words and touch of love.

"Tell me again," she whispered.

He chuckled and stroked her cheek with his finger. "I love you."

"Before or after the Cheyenne wanted to take me?"

"Before. I was coming back to tell you."

She reached up to plant a kiss on his lips, and his beard tickled her mouth. She giggled.

"Looks like I need to take a stand," he said.

"For what?" Had she angered him?

Painted Hands gently righted her to sit alone. "Can I borrow your scissors and your pa's razor?"

She started. "I need to get them from the trunk."

He laughed and hugged her to him. "If I want to kiss you all night, then I'd better be getting rid of these whiskers."

"All night?" Her pulse quickened.

"Until the sun climbs over the horizon."

❧

Painted Hands had worn his beard since the soldiers placed him in the Crandles' home. Full of loathing and longing for his Indian family, Painted Hands chose to blame himself for the tragedies around him. He despised himself so badly that the only way he could cover his shame came in the form of a thick, wiry beard.

"You can hide from yourself, but you can't hide from God," the Reverend Crandle had said.

Painted Hands ignored him, and even when he stepped into the arms of Jesus, he couldn't bring himself to face the truth of his torment. As the years went by, the bitterness deepened until it became like a festered sore eating away at his spirit.

Those days were past. He'd become a new creation. And although he realized the accuser would continue to plague him, he prayed God would always guide him through the tough days.

Sarah Jane held a small mirror beside the lantern while he first cut the beard with scissors, then used the razor. Once he finished, his cheeks felt smooth, like soft buckskin. The exposed areas of his face looked darker, a rather amusing sight. As he further studied the transformation, he noted a peculiar likeness of his face to his hands; both were a mixture of light and tanned skin. Both had resulted in choices he'd made. Suddenly, the scars on his hands weren't so ugly; they represented the love he'd felt for his family and how he'd tried to save them, just as shaving his beard came as a desire not to scratch Sarah Jane's soft face.

"This is strange indeed." He stole a look at Sarah Jane, searching for her reaction.

She gasped. "Painted Hands, you are quite handsome." She reached up and touched his cheek. "I'm glad we married before the other women on the wagon train saw you without your beard."

"I don't remember looking at anyone else but you." His words were void of teasing, for they were true.

"Me?" Her eyes widened.

He set aside the scissors and razor and drew her into his arms. "I thought you had the prettiest color of hair I'd ever seen." He combed his fingers through the curls surrounding her forehead. "It's not red or yellow, as if God had made a special wildflower." He kissed the tip of her nose. "Your freckles remind me of a mischievous little girl, as though I never know what to expect next. And your eyes—many times since we've married, I've been lost in your green eyes, the color of growing earth." From the lantern reflecting from her eyes and adding a soft glow to her skin, she looked lovelier than he'd ever imagined.

"Thank you for making me feel beautiful."

"You are, Sarah Jane, and I've been a fool not to tell you until now. God had to open my eyes to more than one thing today."

⁂

As much as Painted Hands wanted to linger a few days with his precious bride, he saw the foolishness of wasting time with the mountains ahead. The determination to beat the first snows didn't stop him from stealing kisses from Sarah Jane or thanking God for the gift of love. Another concern kept him constantly alert. This was Cheyenne country, and with their allies the Sioux, they ran fear into every white man who embarked upon their land. He'd feel safer once they hit Fort Laramie.

He continued to work on tanning the deer hide by soaking it again overnight. The next day, he flipped it over to scrape off all the hair in the same manner he'd removed the flesh. Today marked the second day for the hide to dry and bleach out on the travois. Not many days from now, Sarah Jane could sew warm clothes for the mountain trek.

On the north bank of the Laramie River, close to where it met the North Platte River, sat Fort Laramie. Painted Hands stopped the wagon to caulk the sides with tar before crossing the river. He hated crossing rivers with a wagon, and the Laramie was a deep and oft times rough waterway. Whereas the lazy Platte seemed to cool off man and beast, the Laramie often plunged into waterfalls.

"I know we're anxious to get to the fort," he said. "But I'm taking the time to construct a raft of sorts. This is one of the most dangerous rivers on the trail."

"Can I help?"

"No, ma'am, but you can watch. Record it in your journal."

She laughed, for it had become his way of teasing her.

She'd much rather record their journey than mend and sew. "All right, and I'll be quiet while you work."

While he labored over the task before him, Sarah Jane wrote what she could before tending to her chores. He never tired of hearing her chat—not at all as he used to.

"Painted Hands, I need to tell you something." She lifted her needle from the pale yellow material.

"You want moccasins, too?" he asked, slinging the axe over his shoulder.

"No, I think boots will be fine. I'm serious. I want to tell you about the money Papa left us so you won't be fretting on how we'll live once we get to Oregon."

"That makes me feel a bit uneasy, Sarah Jane. You should be planning what to do with your parents' money."

"No, it's ours. Anyway, I told you before that Papa wanted to build a mercantile and take advantage of the free land for a farm. We have plenty—we're not rich, mind you, but there's enough for a venture."

He smiled. "I have no idea what we'll do for sure once we get there. From what Reverend Crandle told me, Jacob wanted to start a lumber camp near Willamette Falls, and maybe I could work for him. Then again I might be a farmer. God hasn't told me yet."

She shrugged and commenced to mend again. "I wanted to tell you about the money. Along with selling the cattle, we should be fine."

"Don't you worry about a thing. I'm planning to take good care of you."

She laughed. "I simply wanted to offer something besides another pair of working hands."

"Prettiest hands I've ever seen."

❧

Sarah Jane believed the fifteen-foot adobe walls of Fort Laramie were the most welcome sight she'd seen. It stood as a link to civilization with the Black Hills in the background.

"This is beautiful," she said, drawing the oxen to a halt so she could savor the view. "I wish I knew how to paint so I could keep it forever—to look at it when my mind wandered back to our journey."

"Then memorize every inch of it." Painted Hands rode up close to her. "So someday you can tell our children."

"And our great grandchildren." She'd kept writing in Mama's journal for the same reason. "Do we need many supplies from the fort?" she asked.

"I've taken inventory, and we need only a few. The cost of provisions here is expensive. I used some salt in preserving the deer, and I'd like to replace it. The wheels need repairing but little else. Not sure what kind of price I'll get for the cattle."

"I don't want to stay long." She glanced at him for a response. When he didn't reply, she continued. "I like being alone with my husband."

He chuckled, and she wrinkled her nose at him. The truth was she did prefer his company. Oh, someday she'd want for women-folk talk again, especially when children arrived.

"What's ahead for us?" she asked. "I mean, what can we expect after leaving the prairie behind?"

"The terrain will change, more barren with mostly sage and occasional cedar. Remember the times on the wagon train when we had to stop the cattle before they reached alkali-poisoned water holes?" When she nodded, he continued. "In addition to the water problem, we'll have water holes so full of salt that the animals won't drink it. It's going to be hot and the air thick with dust."

"How hot? Worse than the prairie?"

"Mean, miserable heat. I'm not teasing you about the temperatures. I've seen cattle appear to go mad for water. We're lucky to have only a few to contend with."

"Just tell me what to do," she said. The road ahead would give any woman cause for alarm. She could do it—as long as she refused to think about Mama's fate and the others who had fallen prey to nature's fury.

"Simply endure it, understanding it won't last forever. Once we're through the heat and our skin sunburned, we'll hit Willow Springs. There we can enjoy fresh water and prettier country. I'd like to do a little hunting in that territory. Then we'll follow the Sweetwater River to Independence Rock. A day's travel from there is Devil's Gate and on to the mountains."

She nodded. "I'm ready—prayed up and looking forward to wearing my new clothes. I'll have them finished way before I need them."

"I'm sure every man who ventures into this area wishes his wife would be this excited."

"Those women don't have Painted Hands for a husband. Besides, you're so comely that I'm not so sure I want other women looking at you."

His laughter echoed across the countryside. "Shall I grow my beard to please my jealous wife?"

She stiffened and pretended anger. "You might have to." Then she remembered the cold mountains. "Won't you need it for warmth in the Rockies?"

"Yes, ma'am. But I'll shave it once we're through them."

The bantering, the kisses, the nights snuggled in his arms. Sarah Jane never dreamed her husband could make her so happy. She still had her moments when she missed Mama and Papa; she'd not be a real person without those grieving times. Yet more often her thoughts dwelled on the memorable times with them.

Painted Hands had not said any more about his family and nothing about the years spent with the Kiowa. She would not press him. He'd tell her when he saw fit.

The Greenham wagon train was about two weeks ahead of them, and Painted Hands and Sarah Jane preferred to keep their distance. Once they sold all the cattle but two milk cows and purchased a few provisions, they left Fort Laramie.

There were creeks to cross and lots of time for Sarah Jane to spend with her husband.

In the distance, she saw the vegetation change. A twinge of fear twisted in her stomach. The unknown. The prairie drew her back. Although it had been filled with death and ugliness, it also held her heart. The beautiful, fragrant wildflowers, the blue of the sky, the tall grass that in places soared above her head, and most of all, there she found the love of a good man.

The more she considered this journey to Oregon, the more she realized the trail was filled with uncertainty about the future. She had to trust God; she had no choice.

fifteen

Sarah Jane held her breath at the magnificence of the long, narrow gorge called Devil's Gate. Through the rock flowed the Sweetwater River with cliffs nearly four hundred feet high. She begged Painted Hands to go exploring, for she'd never seen such a magnificent sight.

"I wonder how it was made," she said, staring up at the steep rock.

Taking her hand, he guided her over rocks to the rushing sound of the river. "The Indians have a story if you want to hear it."

"Need you ask?"

He laughed and helped her over a jagged rock. "The Arapaho and Shoshone Indians believe at one time a huge beast lived here and stopped the Indians from hunting and fishing along the river. They decided to attack and kill it, but when they sent arrows into the animal's side, it became angry and tore out the gorge to escape."

"How did you learn this?" Painted Hands always had the best stories.

He shrugged. "Good ears."

"What about the name?" Sarah Jane released his hand and climbed up a rock for a better view of the river.

"I have no idea—probably from the number of people who tried to climb the cliffs and plunged to their death."

She glanced down at the many jagged rocks and decided her husband might be right.

"Leave the climbing to the bighorn sheep," Painted Hands said. "I rather like my wife in one piece."

By mid-August, they reached the Big Sandy. The land

around them held little but sage and the water filled with alkali, but Painted Hands showed her where to find good water and plump gooseberries to vary the everyday diet of biscuits and bacon. Together they ventured across streams until they reached the Green River. From there they ambled in a southwesterly direction.

"The trail to Fort Bridger is desertlike. Remember I spoke about this earlier," Painted Hands said. "Sandstorms and heat that will rival the fire and brimstone one hears from the best of preachers. Wish I knew a better way."

"We've managed before," Sarah Jane said.

He squeezed her hand. "Once we get to the fort, you'll see it sits in a green valley with plenty of water. No doubt we'll need wagon repairs before leaving."

She listened to every word, sealing the terrain in her mind so she could record it later in the journal. More important, she remembered his caution for potential hardships. She would not be a burden to her husband, not now or ever.

Beyond Fort Bridger, a small post with few extra supplies, they moved toward Bear River.

"This is another rough river to cross," Painted Hands said. "The current is swift, even in shallow water."

"I handled the others just fine," she said, although the thought of the wagon tumbling into the water and ruining provisions always frightened her.

"You don't sound so confident."

She offered a faint smile. "I'll not lie to you about it."

An hour later they pulled alongside the Bear. Painted Hands appeared to study its flow. Praise God they'd done this twice before.

"I'll ride the horse across, and you follow me. Take it slow and easy, and we'll get safely across." He glanced at the river, then back to her. "Would you rather take the horse and go first?"

She shook her head and lifted the reins. "I'll drive these oxen."

Painted Hands took the lead, and the oxen stepped into the muddy river. A snake slithered by. Sarah Jane shuddered. The sooner they reached the far bank, the better. The going was slow, and she found herself gripping the reins and praying for courage. At midstream, one of the oxen balked.

She lifted the reins. "Giddyap. Let's get across."

Nothing.

Painted Hands whipped his horse around to help, and he called to the oxen, too.

The wagon started to lean to the right. "Haw! Haw!" she exclaimed in an effort to straighten it.

Painted Hands shouted the same command, but the oxen refused to move. "Jump! Get clear of the wagon!" he shouted.

She doubted if the water was over her head, but she feared the wagon would tip over on her. Her legs wouldn't move. Fear held her in a stranglehold.

"Sarah Jane, jump from the opposite side." Painted Hands's anxious voice rose above her harried thoughts. He urged his horse toward her, splashing water in every direction.

The wagon leaned farther to the right.

"You have to jump!"

She glanced up. *Lord, help me.* It took all of her strength to drop the reins and stand. Any second, the wagon would plunge into the swiftly moving water. Painted Hands shouted at her again. He sounded scared. *I won't be a burden. I won't be a burden.*

She stood and leaped from the left side of the wagon, catching her foot on the side and falling face first into the cold water. She came up sputtering and spitting. Water had filled her nose, and her head stung. She choked and coughed. Painted Hands reached down and pulled her up. In the next instant, the wagon fell. With his hand grasped around her waist, Painted Hands carried her safely to the other side and eased her onto the rocky bank.

"Are you hurt?" he asked.

"No." Glancing back into the river and the toppled wagon, she wiggled free and started back into the river.

"Stop, Sarah Jane. I'll get the wagon," he said. "Stay here."

She shook her head and kept wading in. Tears rolled down her cheeks. "This is my fault." She should have been able to drive the oxen across.

"Get back."

She ignored him until he hurried past her on his horse, and she slipped. Helplessly, Sarah Jane watched Painted Hands calm the oxen, then tie a rope to the wagon and somehow right it and urge the oxen to the other side.

"The food." Her voice came out as a feeble cry. With water dripping from every inch of her, she climbed into the rear of the wagon. The lump in her throat grew larger. They'd starve because of her.

Painted Hands was right behind her. Their clothes were soaked, and their breathing came in quick gasps. The mattress was ruined. Water covered everything. Her fingers clawed over the food. Water-soaked bacon could still be used. Most of the flour lay in a pasty clump, and a large portion of the sugar was dissolved, certain to make everything around it sticky and useless.

"We'll make it," Painted Hands said. "I can hunt, and we can ration what's left. Remember we had more than enough when we started out."

The tears flowed unchecked over her cheeks. "I'm sorry. Please forgive me."

He drew her close. "There's nothing to forgive. What's important is that we're alive, and we'll take care of things and move on." He touched her wet hair. "First thing I'm doing is building a fire so you can dry out. Praise God you were not hurt."

She nodded in a feeble attempt to be brave. Suddenly exhaustion took hold of her, but she refused to give in. "I'll find some wood."

"You'll love Bear Valley," he said, helping her down from

the wagon. His fingers grasped the bones beneath her waist. More than once he'd voiced his concern about her frail frame. "It's as close to paradise as you'll see in these parts. I've tasted some of the best fish and birds you'll ever find. There are wild goat, elk, and deer and so many berries you won't know what to do with them all. I imagine I'll fatten you up for sure."

"How will we make it? What can I do to help?"

"We have a little salt we can use to smoke meat, and in the mountains, the cold will help preserve it all."

❧

Painted Hands lowered his aching back down next to the fire. Tomorrow he'd sit beneath a cottonwood tree and listen to the birds sing—after he'd tended to the many chores facing him. He thought back through the image of Sarah Jane too frightened to jump from the wagon. It could have crushed her. He'd seen it happen on past trips—watched women and children plunge to their death in water far deeper and colder than this. He remembered the wailing of grown men who had lost their families and children. Some were too stunned to cry. With a sigh, he pushed the thoughts away. Sarah Jane was safe. He needn't dig up old memories.

Back at Fort Laramie, some of the old-timers claimed they were in for an early winter, but sometimes weather predictions were stated to frighten travelers. Those who wanted to turn back needed an excuse and used signs of bad weather or threat of hostile Indians to head east. He and Sarah Jane were a few weeks' late moving up the mountain trail, and with the food shortage, he had cause for concern. He decided it was best not to voice his worries to her; she already blamed herself for losing their provisions.

The days and weeks ahead were treacherous. In the past, the Shoshone Indians had helped wagon trains in distress, and the warriors anticipated trading their horses for blankets and knives from the whites. Painted Hands had nothing to barter, but he'd like to hear about the weather farther up in the mountains.

They'd follow the Bear River to the Portneuf River that led to Fort Hall. The fort seldom had anything to offer, being usually short of provisions. From that site, he and Sarah Jane would move along the Snake River for about three hundred miles. This trek was rocky and wild. If his dear wife had been afraid today, she'd be petrified at the steep and narrow trail ahead.

Lord, help me guide us safely through these mountains. I don't have a good feeling about what lies ahead, not a good feeling at all.

sixteen

Sarah Jane had never known such treacherous terrain as that along the Snake River. The oxen tore their feet climbing over sharp rocks, and many times she led the horse while he walked alongside the wagon in case it threatened to plummet down a mountainside. When the trail wove them into the Snake Valley, he steered the wagon clear of deep sand. The blinding dust storms bothered her the most. During those times, she couldn't even see the oxen in front of her. A kerchief and her scarf did little good to halt the cutting grit whipping around their bodies.

Mosquitoes must have been sent from Satan for they settled on the oxen and horse like a fog of torment. Night after night, the horse cried out for relief. Once the sun went down, she and Painted Hands covered themselves completely to avoid the swarming insects. She wondered how many of them they drank in the coffee or ate with their food. Painted Hands led the wagon up the mountain as high as possible to avoid the mosquitoes, but that left them far from the water supply. Leading the animals down a steep path for a mile to secure water, then up again was another arduous task.

Painted Hands and Sarah Jane talked little. Exhaustion took its toll, and when they could take advantage of rest, they were too tired even to mumble a few words. She noted her husband had slipped back into his black moods. He ignored her unless danger prevailed—no smiles or kind words. Some nights she cried herself to sleep, but if Painted Hands heard her weep, he said nothing. She realized he worried about the winter snows and the shortage of food, and when she repeatedly saw his gaze move to the higher mountains, she understood his trepidation. The plunge she'd taken into the Bear River proved how quickly life could be jeopardized.

The journey had to get easier. How could the hardships be much worse?

Twice the Shoshone visited them. They brought salmon and trout, and Sarah Jane cooked it for them all. The friendly Indians appeared grateful—not at all like her dealings with the Cheyenne. She still shuddered when she recalled that ordeal. Painted Hands communicated with them in their own language—something she resolved to learn when time allowed. From what she gathered, the Indians wanted to trade for blankets and knives, but the travelers could spare little. Their new friends no doubt realized the limited amount of food in the wagon. A few times, Painted Hands accompanied them to the fishing streams. While he was gone, Sarah Jane hurried through her chores so she could sleep.

The days blended together in a haze of exhaustion. Her existence with Painted Hands worsened. He resorted to not wanting her to speak, his foul temperament leaving her cold and miserable. She wondered what had become of his relationship with the Lord, but she often felt as surly. She hoped God understood these difficult days. Then the rains came—relentless sheets of water that chilled her to the bone. Some days she thought she'd never be warm or dry again. Her hair froze, but as Painted Hands had claimed, the buckskin suited the purpose more than her dresses. The rocky trails were slick, and she slipped in mud to her knees. At least during the downpours she could cry freely and he never saw.

If only Painted Hands would put his arms around her, hold her as he used to. Some days she wondered if they were growing to hate each other. She wondered if he remembered his previous words of love and affection, for he'd turned more inward than in the days after Mama's and Papa's deaths.

With depression settling around her and no end in sight, Sarah Jane gave up trying to please him. She no longer cared about Oregon or dreams or her husband. Most days she'd have sold her soul for a day of rest and a warm bed. Her whole body ached.

One afternoon, Sarah Jane believed she saw a mirage in the Powder River Valley. The path downward looked every bit as precarious as where they'd come, but the green valley below took her breath away.

"Am I seeing things?" she asked. "Is there really a beautiful valley below?"

Painted Hands grunted affirmation. "Won't last long." He pointed to the snow-capped mountains ahead. "That's what's ahead."

Couldn't he be happy for a small blessing? "Can we rest for a few days?"

"We're already behind."

His granitelike demeanor angered her. "But the animals are worn out. Surely they need to eat for us to continue."

He said nothing in response, but she didn't expect him to.

"Their hooves need time to mend."

His silence angered her. She wanted to scream at him, but she didn't have the strength. His renewed dedication to God and his commitment to her seemed to have vanished miles behind.

"Well, I'm not forcing these oxen beyond the valley until they are rested."

ꝛ

Painted Hands despised the man he'd become. Always the whispers of God urged him to be kind, to be considerate of Sarah Jane. Now, as he helped the oxen down into the Powder River Valley and thought back over his harsh words to Sarah Jane, he realized the truth of why he'd turned back to his black days.

He was afraid.

Simple, forthright, and without a doubt, scared to the point he couldn't think clearly.

For ten years he lived with the Kiowa and learned their ways. He acquired the skills of hunting, surviving in the wilderness, and warfare, but he'd always been with his Indian brothers. With the Reverend Crandle and his wife, Painted Hands learned how to read, write, and ponder the scriptures. From his Indian life to living among the whites, he discovered wisdom and truth. Four times before, he'd journeyed this path to Oregon with the best route, the purest water, food, and survival all sunk into his character.

But he hadn't made the trip to Oregon alone. Greenham led the wagons while Painted Hands scouted for those four trips across the prairies and mountains. Never had he been the sole man responsible for getting the wagons through safely. The fear raged inside him. Every inch of the trek depended on him. He woke in the mornings with a heavy heart at the thought of another day. He loved Sarah Jane so much, but he couldn't look at her or offer a kind word. Her life rested in the palm of his hand, and he refused to take his responsibility lightly.

Not so many weeks ago, Painted Hands believed he was a man, and that man gave his heart to Christ. For the first time in his life, he had felt true peace. With God's gift of love, he treasured Sarah Jane. That part of him seemed like another person.

His prayers for courage and strength went unanswered. He despised his weakness. Sarah Jane had begun to loathe him, and he understood why. In her position, he'd have given up, too.

During the past trips with the wagon trains, he didn't have God directing him. When he realized the importance of a relationship with the Lord of the universe, he embraced Him. Life looked hopeful, especially a future with Sarah Jane. Now fear once more seemed to strangle him.

Taking a deep breath, he glanced back at his wife. Even with dirt woven through her hair and ground into her clothes, she was the most beautiful woman in the world. *Help me, Lord. I hate my heart of stone.*

"We can rest a few days," he said. "These last weeks have been hard on us. I need to wrap chains around the rear wheels to help us over the steep mountain passes, and you're right that the animals need rest."

"Thank you." Her words sounded lifeless, and he ached to make things right between them.

If not for leading the oxen, he'd have walked back to talk to her. But this time, like so many in the past, other priorities took over. If God would take away his fears, then he could be a husband again.

Once the oxen were unhitched and allowed to feed and water, Painted Hands took to repairing wheels and examining every inch of the wagon. The trek across the Blue Mountains usually took four days, and the threat of snowstorms made him want to leave the next morning.

Sarah Jane fished trout from the river and fried it up for supper that night. She hadn't smiled in days, and he knew he was the problem. Sitting beside her on an old log with the fire crackling filled him with a deep longing for the closeness they'd once shared.

"If we had the provisions, this valley would be a beautiful place to stay," he said, feeling the agony of so many wearisome days in his bones.

Her gaze flew to him. No doubt these were the most civil words he'd spoken in too long. He captured her green pools, where once they sparkled like a mountain stream, now dull, dark circles cratered beneath them. "Sarah Jane, I warned you the going would be rough."

"That you did." She closed her eyes and looked around her.

"Saying I'm sorry isn't enough, is it?" he asked.

She continued to study the land about them. "Does it matter?" He heard her release a sigh. "I'm so tired that if I could die this very minute I would."

"You can't give up." He didn't necessarily mean the dreams about Oregon, but also their marriage; except those words stayed on his tongue.

"I believe I have. There's nothing left inside of me but a faint desire to get through another day. The hope is gone. For the first time, I understand how Mama felt."

"And your faith?"

"I'm not sure what faith is anymore." She stood up from the log and massaged her back with her fingertips. "I want to go to bed."

"Sleep until there is no sleep left in you," he said.

"If that were true, you'd need to dig another grave." She left without saying good night. Full of agony, he watched her climb into the rear of the wagon.

"You'll feel better when you're rested," he said.

She failed to reply. Could he blame her when he'd done the very thing to her? He'd turned her against him, destroyed her spirit if not the will to live. The curse lived on.

The next two days, Sarah Jane stayed to herself. She washed clothes, bathed, and roamed the valley. She brought back gooseberries and wildflowers but offered no sign of peace. She looked extremely pale. Painted Hands had seen that look in women before, and he knew the end result. He saw her staring at the mountains and made his way to her side.

"Tomorrow is our last day here," he said. "I see you've taken a liking to the valley. We could spend the morning enjoying what we can of it."

"Go ahead without me." She kept her gaze fastened on the mountains. "I have chores to do."

"The time wouldn't be the same without you." There—he'd said it, the only words of affection he could muster.

"Nonsense, Painted Hands. You much prefer the company of nature to my prattle."

Desperate to find her spunk, he searched his mind for the words to spark some kind of emotion. "We need to get our lives back the way they were."

She tilted her head. "And why is that? Once we start up the mountains, things will go back to the same."

A fall breeze combed through her hair, teasing the reddish-yellow curls that matched the colorful foliage. What he wouldn't give for the music of her laughter.

"I'm sorry for what I've done to you," he said, but she failed to acknowledge him. "Sarah Jane, I wish I knew why I've hurt you over and over again, especially when you are the one person in this world I love. I'd do anything to win you back."

Her blank stare told him all he wanted to know. His morose ways had destroyed their love. And he deserved it.

The trail over the Blue Mountains began with no prayer or formal introduction. Silently, he asked God to guide them safely on to Oregon. The wagon simply climbed higher. Painted Hands remembered when the trees were so thick that he and Greenham, along with other men from the wagon train, had to take axes to hack a path through.

Toward late morning on the second day of the climb, the temperatures fell, and the sky grayed.

"We're in for snow," he said.

She nodded and shrugged. "What do we do?"

"Keep going for as long as we can. If it turns into a blizzard, then we'll have to find shelter."

In an hour's time, the snow started, first in featherlike softness and a rhythmic beauty that in other circumstances would have been beautiful. The intensity increased, and soon it blew fast and furious, reminding him of the tales of lost wagons that had fallen prey to wild blizzards.

"I see a cliff where we can find shelter," he said, pointing. "We'll have to wait this one out."

The snow-roofed rock offered only a bit of reprieve until the heavy fall ceased to blind them.

"I'm going after firewood," he said. "I won't be gone long. Will you be all right?"

For a moment, he saw a flash of something akin to longing. They stood side-by-side, near enough for him to pull her into his arms. "I'll unhitch the oxen and search for wood near the wagon," she said. "I'll have a fire going and food cooked when you return. There're a few kindling pieces in the wagon."

"Stay close, for there isn't much wood nearby. Don't wander off. Keep your sights on the wagon."

Sarah Jane shivered, and he drew her scarf close about her neck. "Later on, when we have a warm fire, I'd like to talk, really talk."

She moistened her chapped lips. If not sun-parched, they were cracked and bleeding from the cold. He wished their love had not taken the same beating.

"Don't fill me with hope again. I can't bear it anymore," she said.

"It's not your doing." Painted Hands touched her cheek with a gloved finger. He thought of telling her about the fear raging through his spirit. He'd missed her, and he wanted what they'd left behind.

Wetness pooled her green eyes. She turned aside and blinked them back.

"Don't you think I know the nights you cried yourself to sleep?"

"I didn't believe you cared." She lifted her face to gaze into his, something she hadn't done in a long time.

He tugged on his scraggly beard. "I never stopped caring, and I'm not sure I can explain it all now."

"You have to try, or we'll never survive."

Painted Hands bent and brushed a kiss atop her head. "I understand."

With the axe on one shoulder and his shotgun slung over the other, he left her feeling warmer than he had all day. The tree line was directly above them, which meant he needed to descend the same path to find fallen branches. Once he gathered a sufficient supply, he'd store them under the wagon.

There they'd dry out, for they might be holed up in the mountains for a while. Painted Hands pushed aside the needling stories of those found frozen to death and focused his attention on the broken limbs below. Some food lay in the wagon, and his shotgun would ward off wolves looking to sink their teeth into the oxen or his horse. He could take down a deer or mountain sheep for meat. They'd be fine for as long as it took.

He shielded his eyes from the snow, then took careful steps downward. Up ahead was a small grove of aspen trees, and farther on he saw pine and spruce. Suddenly, his foot slipped. Reaching down, he tried to stop from gliding down the snow, but he skimmed it like a child's sled on a snow-packed hill. Finding nothing to grab but more snow, he continued to fall. He dare not shout for fear of scaring Sarah Jane. The trees he'd sought loomed his way. Before he could plan how to reach for one and break his fall, his left leg caught on a tree trunk and threw him against another.

Painted Hands heard the snap of his leg, like a tree branch caught under the weight of ice and snow. Sucking in his breath, he assumed the pain would hit him hard, but only numbness met him. He looked to the side. His leg lay twisted in a grotesque shape. He breathed in and out, then attempted to move. And it hit him. A moan escaped his lips with the excruciating pain from his broken leg. Glancing up, he saw the path he'd fallen on was steep, and the way up would be difficult for a whole man.

Swallowing hard, he fought the urge to slip into unconsciousness as easily as he'd descended the mountainside. He stared up at a white sky. Snowflakes dusted his face. He'd be a tasty find for a wolf—along with his wife and animals above him.

I have to find a way to get back up to the wagon.

The means of getting firewood left him defeated. One of his legs felt as if it were on fire, and the other he couldn't feel at all for the cold. He stared at the hand that still held the axe and thanked God he hadn't lost the tool. With it, he had a chance. Surely, in this cold, the pain in his leg might ease up.

I'll crawl up. On the way, I'll think of some way Sarah Jane and I can survive. Oh, Lord, I don't care about myself, but please save my wife.

Painted Hands forced himself onto his belly. He studied the mountain. Somehow he'd make it.

seventeen

Sarah Jane built a fire, using the kindling from inside the wagon and the pieces of wood found not far from the campsite. As Painted Hands requested, she did not venture beyond sight of the wagon, for the snow blew at her back and whirled in front of her eyes. She continued to pick up every stick of wood, whether twigs or bigger pieces, and carry them back to the overhanging rock. Beneath the wagon, they'd dry out, for she assumed they'd be there for a couple of days—or longer. Some of the pieces were large, so she dragged them. Painted Hands could split them when he returned.

She'd admired the trees as they climbed the mountain path: the huge pines varying in size and type of cone, the spruce, the bright yellow foliage of the aspen, the tall fir, the scarlet-and-gold-leafed maple, and the gray-green-barked poplar. She wanted to know about each tree and referred to Papa's traveler's guide to help her identify them.

The afternoon wore on, and Sarah Jane looked anxiously toward the path Painted Hands had taken for wood. Every time she considered looking for him, the snow fell heavier, masking the dangerous downward path. He'd taken the shotgun. Maybe he'd followed fresh tracks of a deer, but as the sun descended to the west, apprehension set before it.

Her spirits lifted, and she sensed calmness in her heart. His parting words were filled with hope, and unless he'd deceived her, he sounded regretful for his actions. And she needed to tell him how the arduous days had darkened her mood. Painted Hands wanted to talk, a promising sign. Where was he now? Would he have gone on and left her alone to starve or freeze to death? She dug through the wagon and pulled out

Papa's shotgun—just in case a hungry wolf took a liking to the animals. And grizzly bears—Sarah Jane rubbed her hands together; she didn't want even to think about wild animals. A moment later, she loaded Papa's shotgun.

The snow stopped. Stepping from beneath the ledge, she scanned the terrain for signs of Painted Hands. Nothing. Her gaze fell on a branch sticking through a mound of white. Every stick of dead wood she could find looked invaluable. During the next several minutes, she pulled and tugged the log to the wagon. Using her foot as leverage, she broke off as many of the smaller branches as possible, moving on to do the same with her other supply. She separated the pine from the other, understanding the soft wood made better kindling. Evening shadows crept across the mountainside. She was hungry but realized the food needed to be rationed, and she'd not eat without Painted Hands.

Hours had passed since her husband first left to gather wood. She stepped as far from the wagon as possible and again searched every portion of the area around her.

"Painted Hands!" Her voice echoed around her. "Painted Hands!"

A branch snapped behind her, and she whirled around to see nothing—and hear nothing more but the rapid beat of her heart. She was utterly alone. Panic seized her mind and mocked her fears.

≈

The hours crept by, and the rush of sunset forced Painted Hands to crawl faster. The slightest movement sent knifelike jabs to his leg and tore at his strength. He clenched the axe in one hand and the shotgun in the other. Slamming the axe into the soft snow, he tried to anchor himself and move another inch, another foot. A glance behind him showed a trail of blood. Wolves would pick up the scent and be on his trail soon. As darkness edged around him, he thanked God for the gun.

His thoughts spun with worry about Sarah Jane. She knew

nothing about surviving in the mountains. At least if she'd been stranded on the prairie, she'd have a chance at survival.

If he died this very night, would she remember he loved her? Would God send someone to help her?

"Painted Hands! Painted Hands!"

His pain-dulled senses thought he heard her calling. He lifted his head and craned his neck, hoping he might be near the top. Quiet. Only the sounds of nature whispered around him. Disappointment nudged him.

Keep going, Painted Hands. Night had not settled on him yet, and as long as he had breath, he'd crawl on to the top.

"Painted Hands!"

He heard her voice again, echoing around him like the cries of a lost child. This could not be the makings of his mind.

He took a deep breath. "Sarah Jane."

Silence nestled in his ears—that and a grim reminder of the pain.

"Painted Hands! Where are you?"

"Sarah Jane, keep talking so I can find you." The effort to shout nabbed his strength.

"I don't see you. Are you hurt?"

Painted Hands heard the anxiety in her voice. "I've. . .broken my leg. I'm crawling up the mountain."

"Help me find you."

He peered about him, looking for something, anything to mark where he lay. "I see three fir trees with a spruce on each side. The trees look like they're forming a tepee. Off to my left is a grove of tall pine."

"I'm looking hard, but the trees seem to blend together."

Her voice sounded raspy as though she were crying or her throat hurt from shouting. "Pray, Sarah Jane." But his words came out like a child's whimper.

"I see you!" she called.

He glanced up, and there she was, making her way down the steep grade, her coat flapping open to the buckskin hugging her body. Never had he seen such a beautiful sight. Tears froze on his cheeks.

Sarah Jane worked her way toward him at a good pace. She planted her feet sideways and half-slid down the slope. Praise God she knew how to move through the snow, even if her experience came from the Nebraska prairie.

"I'm coming. Don't give up on me."

He clung to her words of encouragement. His precious wife had become so thin. Her fragile body could not withstand much more. How would they get the rest of the way up? His gaze stayed fixed on her as he continued to crawl upward with her name on his lips.

When Sarah Jane finally reached him, she wrapped her arms around his shoulders and laid her head against his. He believed an angel had come to deliver him. Indeed, God in His mercy had shown her the way.

"Look at the trouble I've gotten us into," he said in a feeble attempt to sound light. She dare not read his anxiety.

She shook her head and hugged his shoulders. "Well, you didn't dump food into the river."

But I may have carved our tombstones. "We're a fine pair."

"I agree. We have to hurry," she said. "Night is gathering. Tell me how we're going to do this."

"I was hoping you'd have a plan." He shifted his weight and moaned.

"Just to hurry."

"Take the shotgun, and I'll use the axe to make my way up." His leg throbbed with every beat of his heart.

She moved to his right side. "Slip your hand around my shoulders." She grabbed his waist while gripping the shotgun in her left hand. "Do it! Time's a-wasting."

A surge of white-hot fire assaulted him.

"We have to make it up this hill," she said. "We have no choice."

Was it fear that made her insistent? No matter, his wife had her gumption back.

The two crawled up the incline together. When he groaned, she assured him they were almost there; she could see the light from the fire. "I want to get there and add another log," she said. "You need to get warm."

Painted Hands didn't try to talk. It was all he could do to cease his groanings, but the sound came without his realizing it.

"I love you, Painted Hands. We have a life ahead in Oregon."

He hurt too badly to say the same things, so he squeezed the hand holding on to him. Sarah Jane had to ache with the weight on her narrow shoulders.

"I see the fire," she said a few moments later. "I really do. Look ahead. Only a bit farther."

Indeed, they had made it. As much as he hurt, he attempted a laugh.

"Hold on to your sense of humor," she said. "You'll need it when I set your leg."

She'd have to find splints—or make them—and he'd have to tell her how to straighten it. "Tomorrow we'll set it, not tonight."

She nodded, then eased him down beside the fire. Hurrying to the wagon, she came back with a shovel and scooped out the snow that had gathered earlier. In the next instant, she had made a pallet for him. When at last he collapsed on the blankets and she covered him, she picked up the axe and split two logs for the fire. He hated to see her work so hard.

"There's nothing for pain." She sighed. "This will be a bad night for you."

"Not as long as you're here."

She smiled—the one he remembered from their more pleasant days. "I wish I could get you inside the wagon, but this will be warmer."

"The fire is good. Thank you for coming after me. I owe you my life."

She eased over by him. "We're constantly beholding to each other. Let me see your leg and where the blood's coming from."

He turned to see the twisted limb he called his leg. "I

think it's scratched from one of the trees."

Sarah Jane melted snow in a pan, then gingerly dabbed at the gash exposed through his buckskin. In the dancing flames, he saw the weary lines around her eyes.

"Honey, you need to stop. Tomorrow we'll work through the damage I've done today."

She scooted back on her knees and gazed into the fire. "I'm going to treat it; then we should eat. It won't take me long to do either one."

He would not tell her he hurt too badly to taste anything, but both of them needed their strength. Watching her prepare trout that had been caught a few days ago and stayed cold kept his mind off the incessant pain. How beautiful his wife was. He feared this land would take her from him.

"Let's pray before we eat," he said. She took his hand. "Father, You saved me from death today, and I thank You. I also thank You for Sarah Jane. Keep us safe and direct our paths. Amen."

The fish did taste good, but his worries about the future gripped him. He knew the sin of worry, but his thoughts raced ahead despite his spirit's warnings. They'd need firewood and saplings to make a splint. Food was another concern.

"You should try to sleep." Sarah Jane moved to his side and lifted his head into her lap. "Now you have a pillow."

"And what of you?"

"I have what makes me happy at my fingertips." She picked up a blanket warming near the fire and draped it across her shoulders. "Now I not only look like an Indian, but I'll sleep like one."

He feigned a chuckle. "Indians don't sleep sitting up."

"This one does."

Painted Hands slept fitfully that night. The torment in his leg consumed him. The care of his wife overwhelmed him. He prayed; he thought back over his life. God had delivered him too many times for this to be the end, or had he run out of chances? Sarah Jane dozed off from time to time, always waking to see to his needs. They talked little as they simply waited until dawn.

๛

Sarah Jane stood at the crack of sunrise and shrugged the blanket around her shoulders. She split a few logs and added them to the fire. While she made coffee and fried bacon, she listened to Painted Hands explain how to set his leg. The idea of hurting him caused her to tremble, but she pushed the thought aside and concentrated on his directives.

"You'll need three saplings cut the length of my leg and strips of leather or rope to tie the wood pieces to my leg. Pulling it straight is another matter."

After breakfast, she went in search of the wood for splints, making sure she didn't slip on the snow. Her mind raced with the immediate. *How will I put his leg into place? How can I tell if it's straight? What if I don't set it right and he's crippled? When can Painted Hands travel?*

Must life be so incredibly hard?

Snow clouds lingered above, and she picked up her pace. Once she tended to his leg, she'd need to gather more wood. She focused her attention in every direction. If they didn't move on soon, they'd be trapped until spring. Praying for the snow to let up, she hurried her pace. Painted Hands couldn't ride in the wagon over the narrow paths. It was too dangerous.

Everything they'd attempted had been full of peril. Was Oregon worth the price?

At the campsite, Painted Hands lay in torment, but he refused to allow Sarah Jane to know the extent. He swallowed hard and approved of the splints. "The time is now to pull it into place."

Sarah Jane's stomach churned. "How will you stand the pain?"

He nodded toward the wagon. "I'm going to hold on to the wheel. I'd do it myself if I could."

She helped him to the wagon, then carried the sapling pieces and the leather straps and laid them beside him—anything to keep her from completing the task before her. The time had come; she had no more excuses. She cut the buckskin up to his thigh, the gnarled leg a swollen mass of purple and blue. Painted

Hands reached over his head and grabbed the wheel behind him.

"Work fast." Sweat beaded his brow in the frigid temperatures. "You can do it, Sarah Jane. I only wish another man was here to hold me down."

"Help me, Jesus," she whispered. "Dull his pain and guide my hands." She knew better than to look at his face and know her hands caused the excruciating pain. Clenching her fists, she released her fingers and found her hold on both sides of his broken leg. In the next instant, she yanked it into a downward position. Painted Hands jerked and cried out, his voice echoing around them like a hurt animal. Sarah Jane bit her lip until she tasted blood, but she must finish. Seeing the leg needed to be straightened further, she steadied her shaking hands and lined up his leg to match the other.

He gasped, and his face paled. Leaning his head back, Painted Hands closed his eyes. A moment later, he wet his lips and took several deep breaths before looking at the injured leg. "Good," he managed. "Now put the splints in place."

Sarah Jane worked fast, her pulse beating in her head and her fingers trembling like twigs on a dead branch. How could one man endure such pain? When the last leather strap was tied, she stared into his stricken face.

"You did a fine job," he said. "Thanks to you, I'll walk again."

She moistened her lips. "I'll be praying for this leg every morning, noon, and night until we remove those splints."

"I will, too." He closed his eyes and released his hold on the wagon wheel. "Sarah Jane," he said, "when you write about this for our children, don't tell them I nearly cried like a baby."

"I promise. I'll write that you were brave and never uttered a sound." She smiled.

She helped him crawl back to the fire and covered him snugly. Picking up the shotgun and axe, she headed away from the camp. Now she had to find wood.

eighteen

Painted Hands watched her leave until she disappeared in front of a rounded pine. Sarah Jane looked more like a little girl than a grown woman—a grown woman who carried a large burden. How he loved her. She held more strength in her little finger than most men ever achieved. Why she loved him went far beyond his understanding.

He glanced up at the sky; soon the snow would fall again. The old anxieties slapped his face. They'd faced a sad shortage of food before, but with him laid up and the impending weather, the gravity of the situation hit him harder. Helplessness settled on his shoulders.

He couldn't gather firewood; he'd already tried that and failed. He couldn't hunt with a broken leg. He couldn't lead the oxen through the narrow passageways. He couldn't ride his horse. He couldn't clear fallen branches from the trail. In fact, he was totally dependent on Sarah Jane. What irony. The tiny woman he wanted to protect had become his rock. To make matters worse, she was worn out. What if the typhoid attacked her again? For sure, once they reached Oregon, he'd never let her suffer like this.

Dear God, all I can do is trust in Your provision. Show me what I must do.

He exhaled a ragged breath. His leg hurt; the incessant pain offered no reprieve, always reminding him of their predicament. As intense as the agony was, it still didn't compare with her pulling it straight. He'd nearly passed out. He'd even begged God to blacken his mind. Sarah Jane had done a fine job of setting it, and he'd be forever grateful.

The present. He needed to do his share of the work. Until

they were able to move the wagon ahead, they'd need firewood. Painted Hands glanced about. If Sarah Jane was able to find a limb or even a sapling, he'd have a crutch. He realized hobbling around today was next to impossible, but tomorrow. Yes, tomorrow he'd force himself to use a crutch. Being mobile meant he wasn't useless. Another thought occurred to him. He could drive the wagon, and when they reached those precarious places where the wagon risked a tumble over the side of a cliff, he'd limp alongside.

Painted Hands closed his eyes while he waited for his precious wife to return. Last night he lay awake hour after hour waiting for the pain to subside. Today the throb continued. If only he could sleep; a few hours' rest might clear his foggy mind. Maybe then he'd figure out a way to hunt with a crutch or lead the dangerously thin animals down to find grazing. If they died—Painted Hands shook his head and pushed his thoughts in another direction.

Lord, if I was scared before, it doesn't compare with now.

He opened his eyes with a start and realized he'd dozed off. Near the wagon lay a small pile of wood. He managed to smile. She'd left the camp again, but a pot of coffee rested by the fire, just beyond his reach, along with a mug. Dear, sweet Sarah Jane; she always put others first.

He tugged on his leg to help him grasp the mug. An unbidden moan broke the silence, and he fell back.

"Here, let me get the coffee for you," Sarah Jane said, stepping into his view. She carried wood in one arm and dragged a long limb with the other.

"I thought you were gone." He bit on his tongue to keep from crying out.

"I had an idea—something to help you get about." Her cheeks flushed red in the cold. She dumped the wood on top of the other and dropped the limb near him. In the next breath she poured him coffee and delivered it with a kiss. "How are you?"

"I'll live." He smiled at the nearness of her. Odd how love made him forget the danger threatening to take their lives. "Did you bring me that limb for a crutch?" he asked.

"Most certainly. I've been thinking on some other things, too." She sat beside him and drew her knees to her chest. No one ever looked as good as Sarah Jane in buckskins.

"I want to hear every thought."

"I saw two mountain sheep this morning. There's no reason why I can't bring one down." She grinned. "Papa said I had a good eye."

"Sarah Jane, if you can bring in meat, then do so."

She gave him another kiss, this one on his forehead. "And I wonder if I should try to build us a shelter—a cabin of sorts. I'd be slow in cutting down the trees, and I'd need you to tell me what to do."

He gathered her hand into his. "We're asking for trouble to spend the whole winter here. We'd need a solid cabin for that—and a supply of food and wood."

"What else can we do?"

"Find a way to get out of here. You and I will have to switch places for us to get ahead of the weather. I'll take the wagon and you the horse. That's the only way we can make it over the mountains."

Sarah Jane nodded slowly, as if taking in every word and pondering it. A dusting of snow started to fall around the perimeter of their site. "You're saying we'll freeze to death or starve if we try to stay?"

"Yes, and there's nothing here for the animals, either. I want to travel a bit higher above the tree line. At least there we won't have to clear a path in front of us."

She stared into the fire. "I've been wondering if we ought to abandon the wagon. I don't want to, but with the snow and all—"

How much should Sarah Jane suffer? "We aren't at that point yet. We need the wagon to carry provisions and tools.

When we make it to the Columbia River, we'll decide then what's best to do."

"Mama and Papa's things did mean more than I care to admit, but none of it is more important than life." Tiny lines were etched around her eyes.

"I saw women in Independence who insisted upon bringing their fine hats and extra petticoats. Unfortunately, their priorities changed when they faced the hardships of the trail and had to bury a family member. You aren't like any of them, Sarah Jane. You've always known what is important."

She smiled and patted the hand holding hers. "And you see more in me than I really am. When you are ready to leave, I'll ride the mare. I'll try very hard not to give up again; but if I do, please make me go on."

He needed to tell her the truth of why he'd failed her. "I never told you why I turned back to my old ways," Painted Hands said. "It wasn't right. I deserve to be shot for it, and telling you the reason doesn't make things right."

"I did my share," she said. "I ignored you, and when we were in the Powder River Valley, I stayed to myself."

"But you wouldn't have, if not for me. The truth is I was scared, still am, Sarah Jane. I've been on this trail four times, but never by myself. Always someone rode alongside me. Two or three of us made decisions, and we led the wagon train together. Then all of a sudden I realized I was alone. I didn't have the sense to realize I had God as my personal guide."

"I'm sorry. I always thought of you as full of wisdom. I never doubted what you said or what you wanted to do."

He chuckled, moved his leg, then winced. "I'm glad to have your confidence." Having her close did wonders to his spirits. "Have I ever told you any of the tales about other women on the wagon train?"

"No, and I love your stories."

He held onto her hand and stared into her eyes. "Starting out on the trail, I saw women who were so quiet I had to look to make sure they were there; but as the hardships grew, they changed."

"You mean they started not to care about their families?"

"Worse." He took a gulp of his coffee. "Some got mean, spiteful. You could hear them hollering at their children and cursing their husbands. One woman set her wagon on fire. She said if her husband wouldn't take her back across the plains, then she'd make sure they all died."

Sarah Jane's eyes widened.

"Another woman held a shotgun to her husband's head until he pulled out of the wagon line. They never joined back up."

"And I'm sure there were women, like Mama, who gave up." Her sad gaze moved him, and he squeezed her hand a bit.

"For as many folks who make it to Oregon, there are that many graves along the way. You are brave, Sarah Jane. One day our children will tell our story, and you will be praised." He squeezed her hand. "I always appreciated your pa bringing out his fiddle. He made folks forget what was ailing them."

She closed her eyes. "When I'm missing Papa real bad, I think back on him playing a lively tune and Mama laughing. This has been hard, harder than I ever thought it could be, but despite the death and troubles, I'm a better person." She tilted her head. "And I feel as if it's the way God intended for me."

❧

Sarah Jane thought she knew the meaning of fear and believed her worst nightmares came from not seeing the future. Yet setting out on a snow-laden trail with an injured husband and snow flying in her face made her question her sanity.

Now she understood the women in her husband's stories. If not for one hand grasping the horse's reins and the other holding on to God, she'd have said and done more unholy things herself.

Her husband's plan to venture higher might have been easier if not for the wind seemingly pushing them back. Her legs felt so numb that she no longer believed she had any at all. The crunch of snow beneath the wagon wheels said they made some progress, if even a few feet. With a scarf tied around her face, she urged the horse upward, and yet when she looked behind, she could still see their previous campsite.

Have we only moved this short distance? Will we ever climb down from these mountains? The words *God, help us* poured through her mind, spinning around and around lest she forget their true Providence. She turned to see Painted Hands, his face a ghastly white. In her next breath, she gathered the stubborn determination necessary to lead them over the top of the Blue Mountains and on to the Columbia River and the Willamette Valley in Oregon.

When shadows of late afternoon forced them to stop, she was ready to cook a slab of bacon. She'd gone looking for the mountain sheep she'd seen yesterday, but their trail led too far from the campsite, and she was afraid of getting lost. From now on, she must always be ready with the shotgun.

"I think I'd make a good Indian wife," she said in an attempt to ease the gloom. Tomorrow the coffee would be gone. Perhaps she'd boil tree bark to warm them.

"Why is that?" Painted Hands asked through a thin smile.

"I dress like one. I'm learning how to survive in the wilderness, and I haven't thought about a pretty bonnet in weeks. Besides, the Cheyenne warrior thought so."

Her husband lifted a brow. "I think he had other matters on his mind."

She felt her cheeks grow hot, and his laughter bounced off the cliffs surrounding them. "That's what I get for being prideful." Suddenly, she noticed her nose bleeding.

"You're fine, Sarah Jane," Painted Hands said. "It happens when folks are up this high."

She released a pent-up breath and used her scarf to stop the blood's flow. The thought of getting sick and not being able to care for Painted Hands worried her.

"What do we have left in the provisions?" he asked.

If it hadn't been ingrained in her not to lie, she'd have easily done so. "We have frozen berries and a little bacon and a few nuts we found some days ago. A couple of potatoes are left from when we traded with the Indians. There's coffee through tomorrow. No flour or sugar. The cows haven't given any milk for a while." She shrugged. "I promise to do better and try to bring down some meat for us."

"Sarah Jane, soon I'll be able to get around on the crutch. You don't need to feel responsible for keeping us alive. That's my job."

She added a small log to the fire. The wood, too, must be rationed. "I've been so tired of biscuits, but right now, one sure would taste good," she said.

Sarah Jane toyed with the worries in her mind. Surprises were for children. "What are our chances of getting out of this alive?"

Painted Hands's gaze captured hers. "I never believed much in gambling."

"Papa said it was a sin. But he also valued the truth."

"As I said, I never believed much in gambling."

nineteen

The temperature dropped lower that night, and in the morning, Painted Hands and Sarah Jane woke to a blanket of snow. She claimed sleeping by the fire was a much warmer proposition than inside the wagon. Painted Hands understood his wife; she didn't want him alone with a broken leg. As he'd decided before, she carried too much weight on her shoulders.

And their dire circumstances were about to get worse. This morning laid out the dismal truth. They would either starve or freeze to death unless the weather calmed. How far could Sarah Jane venture out from the campsite to gather firewood before they were forced to use the wagon for fuel?

"Let's get going." He caressed her cheek. "Every step we take brings us closer to home." As much as he treasured his heavenly home, he so wanted to reach Oregon with his bride.

She rose from her sleeping position and brushed the snow from the quilt and her hair. "I agree. Shall I fix the last of the coffee?"

Painted Hands hesitated. "I can wait."

She nodded and folded one of the quilts. "I'm not very hungry. We could wait to eat. Maybe even tonight."

You ate so little yesterday. I know what you're doing, Sarah Jane.

"I wish you'd have something now. You need strength for the day," he said.

She stared into his face. Her gaze told fathoms about the anxiety rippling through her. "I'll fry up some bacon and one of the potatoes."

"A wise decision." He took a glimpse of the cattle.

"They can't go on much longer without food," she said. "I can keep melting the snow for water—"

"We'll do the best we can. We need to pray," he said, not taking his gaze from her tired face. "I believe it's time we started."

She knelt beside him, and they bowed their heads. Painted Hands took her hand in his. "God, we need Your help more than ever. We're low on food, and the cattle are growing weak. I'm moving slow, but I'm grateful to be alive. Thank You for Sarah Jane and her courage—and for giving her to me as my wife. Help us to honor You all the days of our lives. We're scared, God, and we're asking for guidance. In Jesus' name, amen."

Her cold lips brushed against his. "He hasn't brought us this far without a plan. We must have faith."

As soon as they had eaten and the animals were watered, Sarah Jane hitched up the oxen, and Painted Hands climbed onto the wagon seat. He'd almost grown accustomed to the pain in his leg.

"We'll make better time if we continue along the tree line," Painted Hands said. "Usually it takes about four days to get over these mountains." *But that is without snow and half a man.* "The valley below is beautiful."

"I look forward to that valley. There we'll rest, and I can fish for food."

Slowly the wagon inched along, the cattle straining against their yoke and the cold wind. Not far was a narrow passageway around the side of the mountain. He'd seen Conestoga wagons too wide to make it around and animals sensing the danger head straight over the side. Praise God for John Benson's wisdom in purchasing a narrow wagon. Still, uncertainty hung in his throat. He had never thought the gut-wrenching fear he saw in men would affect him.

The closer they approached the site where the narrow trail clung to the mountain cliff, the more he realized the need for him to scout ahead. Painted Hands pulled the oxen to a halt.

"I need to see the trail," he said. "Sometimes it's washed out."

"I can do it."

Painted Hands gritted his teeth and climbed down from the wagon. "I can hobble up there."

With the wind crashing against his body, Painted Hands moved upward and around, noting the pathway was clear but slippery. He struggled to maintain his balance, stopping at several intervals to garner his strength. At the steep, angling curve, he breathed a deep sigh of relief that the wagon could round it and start its decline. Now, if the snow let up, they had a chance to make it.

An hour later, Painted Hands stood at the precipice and realized the oxen had to be led. How could he hold onto a crutch with one hand and the oxen with the other?

"I can lead them," Sarah Jane said, as though reading his thoughts. She dismounted. "I'll tie the horse to the back of the wagon with the cows."

"I'll keep the horse with me." He despised the inability to do his share. He'd been over this pass four times and knew the pitfalls. "If the wagon starts to lean or slip backward, get out of its way."

"I learned my lesson the last time," she said.

Alarm registered in his mind. "This is not waist-high water, Sarah Jane. That wagon goes, and you're heading straight down."

She looked at him, startled. "I'll be careful. What about you?"

"I'll hug the side of the cliff."

She moved around to the back of the wagon and climbed inside. A few moments later, she pulled out a dress of her mama's, the Bible with her journal tucked inside, and a box containing the rest of the food. On a second trip, she brought the steel and flint and two boxes of shotgun shells and affixed the other shotgun and rope to his saddle. Inside his saddlebag were more shells. Finally, she carried out the quilts, which she piled beside the box of food. If need be, those could be tied to the horse.

"Have you gotten everything that's important out of the wagon?" he asked, scrutinizing the pile. "What about the axe?"

Sarah Jane shook her head. One more time, she climbed

into the wagon and added the axe, shovel, and bucket to the items on the ground. "I'll come back and get these when we're safely around."

Painted Hands hated to see her work so hard. "I'm serious," he said, pointing to the small mound of supplies. "I can live without any of those things you have there, but I can't live without you."

She took her position with the oxen and started upward. The wagon creaked, and the oxen pulled on the yokes as they plodded forward against the wind and fought to keep from sliding backward. From where he limped in the rear nearest the cliff, it seemed headed for the sky. If there had been more wagons, they'd have used men and chains to pull each one up.

Slowly, they ascended to the top. Painted Hands forgot about the pain in his leg. He kept one eye on the wagon and the other on Sarah Jane. Each step became a prayer for the chains to dig into the slippery snow. He felt cold to the bone, but sweat dripped down the side of his face.

When at last they made it around the curve, the incline lay before them more menacing than the trek up. Painted Hands studied the trek down.

"Stay clear." Painted Hands had not felt so helpless since the childhood fire.

The moment the wagon started to slip, he shouted for Sarah Jane. He saw the tragedy coming, but he couldn't get to her fast enough. Painted Hands quickened his pace, slipped, and braced his fall.

"Sarah Jane, get out of the way. You can't stop the wagon."

She cried out to the oxen. But the wheels spun faster, and the wagon gained momentum, heading straight down the pass. Sarah Jane screamed.

Then he saw her, kneeling on the rock hard ground, her face buried in her hands. In the next instant, the sound of the wagon and frightened animals crashing against the side of the cliff reverberated around them.

"It's all right," he repeated as he hobbled to her side. "You're safe."

Once he reached her, Painted Hands dropped the crutch and eased down beside her, holding her sobbing body next to his.

"I'm sorry," she managed, burying her face in his chest. "I tried. I really tried."

"You did better than any man, ten men."

"Twice I've failed."

He kissed the top of her head. "Twice you've escaped death. That's what's important."

"What will we do now?" she asked between sobs.

Painted Hands took a deep breath. "We're going to head down this mountain, put our supplies on a travois, and lead the horse to Oregon."

⌖

Sarah Jane was cold, colder than she could ever remember, and she sat in front of a fire. Her eyes stung, and her head ached. No matter how hard she rubbed her hands together, they refused to thaw. She kept wiggling her toes for fear they'd be frostbitten. She and Painted Hands drank the last of the coffee and ate a little of the bacon. When her teeth chattered, he wrapped his arms around her and suggested she remember the heat on the prairie. Perhaps the memories would warm her body, but nothing helped. Sarah Jane wanted to cry, although it clearly upset him when she wept.

They couldn't hold out much longer. Traveling down the mountain was slow with Painted Hands limping on his crutch. He tried to move faster, but it hurt him so. If their days were numbered, then they needed to talk about their lives before they married. Sharing joys and sorrows sealed their love—even in death.

"I'd like to hear about the years with the Kiowa," she said, studying his face. "I see you cared for them very much."

His gaze softened. "I did. They became my family when I no longer had one. When the hunting party brought me to the village, I was scared. I grieved for my family, believing their deaths were my fault. My hands were badly burned, and in my mind, I deserved the pain. A Kiowa couple took me in. The woman coated my hands in a type of salve and wrapped them in cloth. At night, when I cried for my family, she held me. Later on, I learned she'd lost a son in a fire, and I became her replacement. All the love she had for him was now mine. When the other children teased me about my hands, she ran them off. She gave me the name of Painted Hands and told me I should be proud. I had fought the fire and won. The scars were a symbol of honor, and I should never be ashamed of them."

"A wise woman, Painted Hands."

"Her husband treated me like his own son. He taught me how to hunt buffalo and to show courage in battle. He was a member of the Koitsenko, one of the ten most highly respected warriors in the tribe. I remember he wore a red sash around his waist and carried a sacred spear when he went into battle. Those were the days when the Cheyenne and Kiowa were fierce enemies, and those warriors knew how to fight."

She gasped. "They could have killed you that day on the prairie."

He pressed his lips together and said nothing for several moments, as though his memories had carried him back to before the days of their marriage. "The two tribes made a peace treaty about eight years ago, and we're both lucky they honored it, especially since I'm white."

"How were you trained to show courage?"

He grinned. "By proving myself as a hunter and achieving war honors."

"Do I want to know about the war honors?"

He chuckled, the first time he'd laughed in a long time. "I stole a few horses from the enemy and charged their warriors in battle." He paused. "I was happy, content with life. I followed the many gods of the Kiowa and consulted the medicine men for guidance. My white parents had instilled the teachings of the Bible, but everything in that life had died. I no longer felt as if I belonged in the white man's world, neither did I want to. But still I had the nightmares about the fire."

Sarah Jane struggled to understand. "You didn't long for your own people?"

"I was a little boy who craved love and family. From the Kiowa, I learned respect and what it meant to be a respected warrior of honor. After ten years, the white man's ways were foreign."

"How did the soldiers find you?"

"Another man spotted me in a hunting party, and the soldiers rode out in search. None of them bothered to ask me if I wanted stay."

"They took you against your will?"

He nodded. "The soldiers surrounded the hunting party and at gunpoint singled me out. I put up a good fight, but there were too many of them. I used to wonder why they found me so easily, but now I realize it was part of God's plan. They brought me to Independence, and the Reverend Crandle and his wife took me in."

"Weren't they afraid of you?"

"Sarah Jane, I would have slit every white man's throat within miles if given the chance. The soldiers brought me tied up like an animal to the Crandles, but as soon as they were gone, the reverend spoke kindly to me and cut me loose. He told me that if I wanted to go back to the Kiowa, he'd let me go, but he asked for a chance to show me the white man's way of living. I don't know why I agreed, except the Reverend Crandle trusted me not to hurt him. Two years later, I overheard a soldier telling him that most of my Kiowa village had been killed. It took a lot of talking on the reverend's part to convince me not to seek revenge.

"He's a great man of God. He believed in me when I gave up on myself. He taught me how to read and write and to trust God, not man. Unfortunately, it has taken me a long time to find the faith he lived. I'm not sure how he found out about Jacob. All I know is he met with him while I was on the trail with Greenham."

She rubbed her hands over the fire. "Oh, but you will. Once we get to Oregon, you two will be inseparable."

His face darkened. "I hope so. I pray so." A moment later, he glanced up at the sky lit with a thousand twinkling stars. "You had a good life with your folks?"

"For the most part, yes. Papa was a dreamer with grand plans. He laughed a lot and always had something witty to say. At least I thought his words were worth remembering. He always wanted something better for us, while Mama wanted to stay in the same place and be happy with what we had. At times they quarreled about it, especially when Papa sold the farm and moved us to Independence. Mama missed her friends, and living in a wagon did not sit well with her. The worst time between them happened when Papa decided we were going to Oregon. She cried and begged him to let us live in Independence. They talked things out right before she took to feeling poorly. They loved Jesus and understood the importance of following Him. I'm thinking all marriages have their mountains and valleys."

"We've had ours. The mountains can be a little cold, though." She managed a laugh.

He squeezed her a little tighter. "You're too thin. I'm afraid this wind will blow you away."

She was tempted to give in to the gloom, but she refused. "When we get to Oregon, I'll eat everything in sight. Most likely get fat. Then we'll have babies, and I'll get fatter."

"Babies," he whispered. "I'd like to be a father."

"Good, 'cause I want to be a mother."

"We can't give up, can we, Sarah Jane?"

She shook her head and swallowed the lump stopping her from speaking.

"I love you more than I ever thought possible." The gentleness in his voice made it even more difficult to hold her composure. "For as long as God gives us, I will be devoted to you," he said.

No longer able to keep her emotions hidden, she turned to him and buried her face in his chest. "You would have made it to Oregon if not for me. Dying up here is my fault. I'm so sorry."

"No one is to blame. We're part of God's plan, and I believe we will survive. Every step we take down brings us closer to warmer weather and a supply of food."

A wolf howled, then several more. Normally, their presence meant little to her when she sat in front of a fire. But tonight, in facing the bleak outcome of cold and starvation, the wild animals frightened her. For a moment, she allowed the comforts of home in Nebraska to soothe her. Perhaps she needed to dwell on the promises of heaven instead.

twenty

Another day's trek downward, and Painted Hands grieved with the slow progress. Four days over the mountains had turned to seven. Too often he had to stop and rest. The slippery incline and the debris that covered the path made the going difficult. The food was gone; Sarah Jane hadn't wanted to tell him about the shortage, but he saw the diminishing provisions. Hunting with his broken leg seemed nearly impossible unless an animal walked in front of him, and the idea of sending his wife out into the wilderness sounded just as menacing. They could melt snow for water, but how long could they continue without food?

Snow clouds loomed overhead. Everywhere he turned, life dealt another blow. *Why, Father? I'm trusting You, but our future looks grim.*

In the next hour, the snow started. The two walked as far as they could until the whirling white mass blinded them. They were forced to find shelter, this time under a pine tree. Sarah Jane gathered wood, and he started a fire. His stomach rumbled as it had for days. Tree bark had begun to look good.

Huddled together, they watched the snow drift and blow, each flake sealing their future. He'd lost all hope, but he dare not tell Sarah Jane. He melted snow over the fire and offered it to her, but she refused. Their destiny was freezing to death or starvation, whichever came first.

"Talk to me," Sarah Jane said, snuggling closer. "I'm sleepy and can't get warm."

"Drink the warm water."

"I can't. I want to sleep."

"Stand up. Move around. Jump up and down." He tried to chase away the panic from his voice by replacing it with anger, but even he doubted his tone.

"No, I can't. I'm too tired."

He heard the resignation. "I won't let you give up. What can I do?"

"Tell me a story. I want to fall asleep listening to your voice."

His mind registered nothing. He couldn't remember anything. If she'd been a man, he'd pick a fight. "As your husband, I'm telling you to stay awake."

"It doesn't matter. I can't go on." Her weak voice sent a streak of fear through him.

"But you must. We can wait out this storm and go on." Painted Hands searched for the words to keep her awake. "I'm asking for a favor, Sarah Jane. Look at me with those beautiful green eyes and call me by my given name."

He felt her frail frame shiver, and she positioned herself to face him. "Toby."

"Do you like the name?"

"Oh, yes. It's pleasing to the ears." Her voice grew fainter.

"I want to name our first son Toby. What do you think of that?" His mind raced. Whatever it took, he could not let her fall asleep. *Please, God, slow down the snow. Let us walk down this mountain.*

"We won't have any children. We are going to die right here."

"No!" He shook her. "We are not."

"Please, Painted Hands—"

"The name is Toby." He shook her again.

"It's no use. Just let me be."

He felt tears and anger spur him on. "I thought you were your father's child. Fight this, I beg of you! Stand up and move."

She slumped against him. "I'll try." Slowly, she rose to her feet. She lifted her arms to the sky and wiggled them, then fell beside him. "It's too hard."

"All right, we'll talk. I want to name our children, a dozen of them. The first son is Toby. What will we call our first daughter?"

She sighed. "Lydia Jane, after my mother."

"Good. Another son we could call John William after your pa."

She nodded and relaxed against him.

"And another girl named after you and my mother—Sarah Elizabeth." When she didn't reply, he nudged her. "Sarah Jane, talk to me."

She didn't answer; her eyes were closed. He wanted to give up, too, but his thoughts raced in prayer. Only God could deliver them—either into His hands for eternity or through a miracle.

⋇

Painted Hands woke with a start. He had no concept of time, only that the light glistening off the snow caused him to blink. Flames from the fire soared as though reaching up to the sky. It warmed him to the bone. How had this happened? Buffalo robes covered them. He glanced at Sarah Jane sleeping in his arms. She looked like an angel at peace, and a faint smile etched her delicate features. Her chest rose and lowered. He kissed her forehead, then her lips. Praise God she still lived. But who had stoked the fire?

Then he saw them. Three Cayuse Indians, a tall race who moved with grace and agility. They were dressed warmly in shirts, fringed buckskin, buffalo and deer robes. One brought out dried salmon and breadlike cakes made from camas bulbs. Painted Hands stared up. He hoped the gratitude shone from his eyes, because he didn't have the strength to pull out his arms to talk to them in sign language.

Cayuse Indians. Less than a year ago, in November 1847, they had killed Marcus and Narcissa Whitman and twelve others at the Whitman mission. Growing resentment that the whites intended to take over the Cayuse land escalated when a measles epidemic broke out and killed many of the Indians. They feared the whites had brought the disease to destroy the Indians. They blamed those at the Whitman mission and took revenge. Why were they helping him and Sarah Jane now? The reason didn't matter, only that they were there. This wasn't the first time God had sent Indians to deliver him.

Painted Hands attempted to move about. A Cayuse who wore a horned headdress handed him a cup of hot broth. It tasted of deer and root vegetables, like the finest of food. Slowly, his head began to clear as his body thawed. A short while later, he pulled his arms from beneath the buffalo robe and signed his gratitude to the four sitting beside the fire.

"We are glad to have found you," said the one who had given him the broth.

Odd how the Indian spoke perfect English. Perhaps he'd learned from the Whitmans.

"My wife and I had given up, believing only God in His providence could save us," Painted Hands said.

"God has answered your prayers." He pointed to Painted Hands's broken leg. "Your leg has been set straight. I believe you will walk upright when it heals."

A strange sensation settled on the back of his neck. By all rights, he and Sarah Jane should be dead, either from the cold, the starvation, or the Cayuse—Indians who spoke excellent English and waged war against the whites. None of this made sense. Perhaps this was a dream or a passageway into heaven.

"How did you find us?" Painted Hands asked. He felt no fear, but he *should*.

"We found the remains of your wagon and searched you out," the Cayuse replied.

"I will be forever grateful."

"We will take you to the river. From there you can take a canoe to the white man's settlement."

"Why didn't you kill us? Have the Cayuse agreed to peace?"

"Your God led us to you. We respect His power."

In awe of what God had done through these Indians, Painted Hands realized no works of man, neither good nor evil, could stop God's purpose. Many would never believe this wondrous story, except those who had also experienced a miracle.

"I wish I had something to give you in return," Painted Hands said.

"A prayer for our people is enough. We fear the whites will kill us all, and yet we must fight for our way of life."

"I will pray for you as long as I have breath." Painted Hands understood the plight of these Indians, just as he'd understood the troubles of the Kiowa, Cheyenne, Pawnee, Sioux, and all the other Indians who faced the overwhelming odds of the whites seeking to occupy the Indians' lands. He saw both sides, and it grieved him.

"Your heart is good," the Cayuse said, his voice strong yet gentle. "Your wife, she must eat, too."

"Wake up, Sarah Jane." He kissed her forehead. "We have been delivered."

⁂

For the next four days, Painted Hands and Sarah Jane stayed with the three Cayuse Indians. The couple regained their strength, then started down the mountain with the Indians guiding them. Some of the trails were familiar to Painted Hands, but others were only wide enough to accommodate a walking path. The Indians provided horses and food every step of the way.

"Where is their village?" Sarah Jane asked while they rode horses the Cayuse provided.

"I asked the one who wears the horn headdress, but he did not answer."

"I am amazed you speak their language, too," she said with a smile. "You are constantly surprising me."

Painted Hands was startled. "I don't speak their tongue. They speak English."

Sarah Jane peered at him oddly. "But I never heard English—it was something else."

Painted Hands realized another miracle had taken place. Forever, he'd praise God for blessing him far beyond what he deserved.

"Where are they taking us now?" she asked.

"To the Columbia River, where we'll take a raft all the way to the Methodist mission at the Dalles. The rapids are horrible, but God has brought us this far—and He will see us on to the Willamette River and the Willamette Valley."

"And to Jacob," she said. "Do I continue to call you Toby?"

He thought for a minute. "I am a white man who has been delivered by God through the Indians of this vast country time and time again. I'm proud of my experience with them, but I am Toby Carlson."

She reached out for his hand. "I'm so proud to be your wife. I love you no matter what you choose to be called."

"And I'm blessed to have the love of a fine woman."

On the shores of the sparkling Columbia River, the Cayuse helped Toby construct a raft. When completed, Toby and Sarah Jane bundled their few belongings together and turned to the Indians.

"Thank you again," Toby said, hearing his words swell with emotion. "You saved our lives." He grasped the shoulder of the man wearing the horned headdress—the one Toby called friend.

"Remember to pray for our people." The man smiled.

"I give you my word. I do not even know your name."

"Names are of no purpose when God calls us brothers."

"I understand." Toby stared into the man's dark eyes. Peace and warmth radiated from the dark pools.

"Your leg will heal without a limp." The man paused. "God has healed your heart and your body. Show to others what He has done for you."

Toby nodded and swallowed hard. "God bless you, my friend and brother."

The Cayuse turned, and the men disappeared into the trees. Toby wrapped his arm around Sarah Jane. "God's ways are mysterious," he whispered and planted a kiss on her forehead. "With His guidance, I will never return to my black moods. I am a free man who knows his source of strength."

Sarah Jane leaned her head upon his chest as he balanced on his crutch. The rush of water whirled around them. "I am not afraid of what's ahead."

He pulled her closer. "Neither am I."

epilogue

"Toby, how will we know it's Jacob?" Sarah Jane asked. Her gaze flitted from one man to another among the small crowd in Oregon City.

"I don't know. Maybe I should be carrying a sign stating: Looking for Jacob Carlson." He, too, searched all around them. Men, women, and children went about their business. "I wish I knew if he had a wife or what he looked like. We'll ask for the nearest logging camp, talk to everyone we meet, and keep looking until we find him."

Sarah Jane held her breath. There, not ten feet in front of them, stood a man who looked identical to Toby: the same walnut-colored hair and beard, the same broad shoulders and stocky build. She tugged on Toby's sleeve. He turned to the man.

"Jacob?"

The man stepped forward with outstretched arms. "Toby."

The two enveloped each other in hugs and laughter.

Jacob stood back and shook his head. Tears streamed down his face. "I've prayed twenty-three years for this day. I heard from a Charles Greenham that you'd been left behind on his wagon train. Since that day, every time I got word of new emigrants making their way into Oregon City, I've been here."

Toby wrapped his arm around Sarah Jane's waist. "This is my wife, Sarah Jane."

Jacob first grasped her hand, then pulled her into his arms. "Welcome, my sister. If the good Lord took me home this hour, I would live in gratitude for seeing Toby and his bride before me today."

"Thank you." Tears trickled down Sarah Jane's face, and she

quickly whisked them away.

"We have years to catch up, little brother." Jacob turned to Toby and laughed long and hard. "I have so much to tell, and I want to hear about the years you spent with the Kiowa."

"When can we get started?" Toby asked. He paused and nodded as though pleased with life and everything in it.

"Tonight," Jacob said. He grasped Toby's shoulder. "And what are your plans now that you are here?"

Toby shrugged. "To find work, maybe farm."

"I could use a partner at the beginnings of a lumber camp—if it suits you."

Sarah Jane felt her emotions rise to the surface. She knew Toby's desire to work with his brother.

"That would suit me just fine. God does listen to the prayers of the heart," Toby said. He gazed into Sarah Jane's eyes, then looked at Jacob. "He's answered every one of mine."

A Letter To Our Readers

Dear Reader:

In order that we might better contribute to your reading enjoyment, we would appreciate your taking a few minutes to respond to the following questions. We welcome your comments and read each form and letter we receive. When completed, please return to the following:

Fiction Editor
Heartsong Presents
PO Box 719
Uhrichsville, Ohio 44683

1. Did you enjoy reading *Kiowa Husband* by DiAnn Mills?
   ❏ Very much! I would like to see more books by this author!
   ❏ Moderately. I would have enjoyed it more if

   _____

   _____

   _____

2. Are you a member of **Heartsong Presents**? ❏ Yes ❏ No
   If no, where did you purchase this book? _____

   _____

3. How would you rate, on a scale from 1 (poor) to 5 (superior), the cover design? _____

4. On a scale from 1 (poor) to 10 (superior), please rate the following elements.

   ____ Heroine   ____ Plot
   ____ Hero   ____ Inspirational theme
   ____ Setting   ____ Secondary characters

5. These characters were special because?_____

_____

_____

6. How has this book inspired your life?_____

_____

_____

7. What settings would you like to see covered in future
   Heartsong Presents books? _____

_____

_____

8. What are some inspirational themes you would like to see
   treated in future books? _____

_____

_____

9. Would you be interested in reading other **Heartsong
   Presents** titles? ❑ Yes ❑ No

10. Please check your age range:
   ❑ Under 18   ❑ 18-24
   ❑ 25-34   ❑ 35-45
   ❑ 46-55   ❑ Over 55

Name _____

Occupation _____

Address _____

City_____ State_____ Zip_____

FRONTIER BRIDES

4 stories in 1

Four romances ride through the sagebrush of yesteryear by Colleen L. Reece.

Reece shares the compelling stories of people who put their lives on the line to develop a new land. . .and new love.

Historical, paperback, 464 pages, 5 ³/₁₆"x 8"

Hearts♥ng

Presents

Great Inspirational Romance at a Great Price!

Heartsong Presents books are inspirational romances in contemporary and historical settings, designed to give you an enjoyable, spirit-lifting reading experience. You can choose wonderfully written titles from some of today's best authors like Peggy Darty, Sally Laity, Tracie Peterson, Colleen L. Reece, Debra White Smith, and many others.

When ordering quantities less than twelve, above titles are $2.97 each.
Not all titles may be available at time of order.